three beds
in manhattan

also by georges simenon

translated from the french by
lawrence g. blochman

georges simenon

three beds in manhattan

doubleday & company, inc.
garden city, new york
1964

First published in France under the title
TROIS CHAMBRES À MANHATTAN.
Copyright 1946 by Georges Simenon.

Library of Congress Catalog Card Number 64–10560
Copyright © 1964 by Georges Simenon
All Rights Reserved
Printed in the United States of America
First Edition in the United States of America

three beds
in manhattan

chapter 1

At three o'clock in the morning he couldn't stand it any longer. He got up and started dressing. At first he considered going out in his slippers, without a tie, and with the collar of his overcoat turned up, like the dawn and midnight dog-walkers, but thought better of it. When he reached the courtyard of this house, which even after two months he could not bring himself to look upon as home, he glanced up and saw that he had forgotten to turn out his light. Well, let it burn; he didn't have the courage to climb the stairs again.

He wondered how far along they were, up there, in J.K.C.'s apartment, next to his. Had Winnie started to vomit yet? Probably, accompanied by groans, softly at first, then louder. She would wind up with an interminable fit of sobbing.

As his footsteps echoed in the nearly empty streets of

Greenwich Village, he was still thinking of those two who had once more wrecked his sleep. He had never seen them. He did not even know what the letters J.K.C., painted in green on the door next to his, stood for. He had noted one morning through the half-open door that the floor was painted a glossy black, which made the bright red furniture all the more startling.

He knew a few fragmentary facts about the couple, but he could not link them together to make sense. He knew, for instance, that J.K.C. was a painter, and that Winnie lived in Boston. He could not imagine, however, what possible profession allowed her to come to New York on Friday evenings only, on no other day of the week, and never for a whole weekend. She always came by taxi a few minutes before eight o'clock, apparently from the train terminal, for the time never varied.

Winnie's voice was sharp and piercing when she arrived; she put on her second voice later. Combe could hear her walking back and forth as she talked with all the volubility of a new arrival. Then they would dine in the studio. Every week the dinner would be delivered from an Italian restaurant a quarter of an hour before the girl came.

J.K.C. talked little and in muffled tones. Despite the thinness of the walls, he was almost impossible to understand. On the other evenings, when he telephoned to Boston, only an occasional phrase came through. And why was it that he never telephoned before midnight, sometimes long after one in the morning?

"Hello. Long-distance . . . ?"

And Combes would know that he was in for a long session. He always understood the word "Boston," but he never caught the exchange. J.K.C. called person to person, so Combe knew that the girl's name was Winnie, but could not hear her last name. It began with a *P*, apparently, and had an o and an l in, but that was all that came through—except the long, muted murmuring that followed.

It was exasperating, but not so exasperating as the Friday evenings. What did they drink with their dinner? Something strong, no doubt, which they drank neat. Winnie's voice quickly lost pitch and gained resonance, and Winnie lost all restraint and inhibitions. Combe would never have imagined that passion could produce such unbridled, animal-like violence.

And all the while the unknown J.K.C. remained calm and self-controlled, speaking in soft, even tones that seemed touched with just a trace of condescension.

After each new tempest she demanded more to drink, and Combe could picture the studio a shambles, with fragments of the broken glasses glittering on the glossy black floor.

Tonight Combe had gone out without waiting for the inevitable sequence, the hurried trips to the bathroom, the hiccups, the retching, the vomiting, the tears, and finally the endless wail of a stricken animal—or a hysterical woman.

Why did he continue to think of her? Why, as a matter of fact, had he left his room? He had been promising himself that one Saturday morning he would manage to be in the hallway or on the stairs when she left. No matter how stormy the night, she always awoke at seven. She needed no alarm clock. She didn't even wake her artist friend, for there was no sound of voices. There were only vague sounds in the bathroom, perhaps a kiss on the forehead of the sleeping J.K.C., then the door would open and close softly. Combe could imagine her quick steps on the sidewalk as she ran for a taxi to take her to the terminal, but he could not decide how she would look. Would the wild night have left its traces on her face, a droop to her shoulders, a huskiness in her voice?

It was the morning woman he would have liked to see, not the evening woman, just off the train, full of poise and self-assurance as she swept into the studio as if she were dropping in on casual friends. Yes, he was interested in the morning woman, who stole off alone into the awakening day, while the man slept on in his selfish calm, unaware that his clammy forehead had been brushed by a kiss. . . .

Combe had been walking aimlessly. He came to a corner that was vaguely familiar. A night club was closing, its last-gasp customers spewing out to the curb, optimistically waiting for taxis. Two men at the corner apparently could not bear to say good night to one another; they parted, shook hands again, parted again, and came back drunkenly to reaffirm everlasting friendship.

Combe suddenly felt that he too had just emerged from a night club instead of a warm bed. He was strangely exhilarated, although he had not had a drink all evening. Instead of the caressing warmth of night-club music, he had spent the evening in the cold loneliness of his room, made even lonelier by the love cries that filtered through the wall.

He forced himself to the reality of his street corner. A yellow cab had finally stopped in front of the night club, had been assailed by a dozen prospective fares, and had escaped with difficulty—but empty. The street lights festooned the almost deserted avenues with their garlands of softly glowing globes. At the corner a brilliantly lighted show window thrust itself aggressively into the half-gloom, a long glass cage that vulgarly challenged the dark human shadows on the sidewalk to bring their loneliness inside. Combe went in.

He surveyed the stools anchored in front of the endless counter of cold plastic. He watched two drunken sailors trying to bid each other good night with much handshaking and unintelligible language. He slid onto a stool without realizing that he had taken a seat next to a woman. A white-coated Negro counterman stood in front of him, waiting for his order. He looked around. The place smelled of the morning after, of dead carnival, of night people who can never make up their minds to go to bed; it also had that curiously typical New York smell of quietly impersonal nonchalance and brutal individualism.

He ordered at random—grilled sausages. Then he turned to look at his neighbor. The counterman had just slid a platter of bacon and eggs in front of her, but she ignored the food, calmly returning Combe's evaluating glance. She took her time lighting a cigarette, then carefully examined the imprint of her rouged lips on the tip. Then:

"Are you French?" she asked in French—without an accent, he thought at first.

"How did you guess it?"

"I don't know. I sensed it as soon as you came in, even before you spoke." With a nostalgic smile she added, "Parisian?"

"Parisian indeed—from Paris."

"Which quarter?"

His eyes grew misty for an instant; he wondered if she had noticed it. "I had a villa in Saint-Cloud. Do you know Saint-Cloud?"

She smiled and, imitating the monotone of a dispatcher for the Seine river boats, she announced, "Pont de Sèvre, Saint-Cloud, Point-du-Jour . . ." Then, lowering her voice, she said, "I lived in Paris for six years. Do you know the Auteuil church? My apartment was practically next door, at the corner of Rue Mirabeau, a few steps from the Molitor swimming pool. . . ."

He was listening, but he was trying to relate this

throwback from Paris to the reality of a night in New York. How many people were there in this all-night coffee pot? Perhaps a dozen, separated not only by empty stools but by an emptiness that was difficult if not impossible to define, an emptiness that seemed to emanate from each of the customers. They were linked only by two Negro waiters in soiled white coats who made frequent trips to a hole in the wall from which they extricated plates containing hot edibles of some sort, which they slid along the counter to some anonymous but hungry character.

In spite of the blazing lights, there was a pall of grayness hanging over the lunch counter, a bleak loneliness that defied the glare. The blinding neon tubes might hurt the eyes, but they could not dissipate the night that these men brought in with them from the outer darkness.

"Aren't you eating?" he asked, chiefly because the silence had become embarrassing.

"I'm in no hurry."

She smoked the way American girls smoked in magazine ads and in the movies: the same pout of the lips, the same angle of the wrist, the same way of throwing her fur back from her shoulders to show her black silk dress to advantage, the same way of crossing her sheer-sheathed legs.

He had no need to turn toward the girl to catalogue her fine points. There was a long mirror that ran the length of the counter so that they could look straight ahead and see their images sitting side by side. The reflections were certainly unflattering, and perhaps even a little distorted.

"You're not eating either," the girl said. "Have you been in New York long?"

"About six months." Why did he find it necessary to introduce himself? A touch of vanity, naturally, which he regretted as soon as he had said, "I'm François Combe."

Perhaps he had not said it with the easy grace he had

intended. In any case, she did not seem impressed—even though she had lived for six years in Paris. Strange . . .

"Were you living in Paris recently?" he added.

"Let's see . . . Not for the last three years, really. I passed through on my way from Switzerland, but I didn't stop long." After a brief pause she added, "Have you been in Switzerland?" Then, without waiting for a reply, she continued, "I spent two winters in a sanatorium in Leysin."

Her last words made him look at her for the first time as a woman. Before he could analyze his reaction, she went on with a superficial gaiety that touched something deep inside him.

"It's not as terrible as people think. Not for those that get out, anyhow. They told me I was definitely cured."

She crushed out her cigarette in an ash tray and again he looked at the bloodlike stain of her lipstick. Why, in that fraction of a second, did his thoughts revert to the Winnie he had never seen? Perhaps it was because of her voice. He had not noticed it before, but this woman, whose name he did not know, did indeed have a voice like Winnie's—but the Winnie of the tragic moments, the Winnie of the lower, sonorous voice, the Winnie of the wounded animal.

It was like Winnie's voice, but different—more subdued, perhaps, more muted, like a scar that was not quite healed, a pain that lies constantly below the conscious, but that remains a cherished part and parcel of oneself. . . .

She had just ordered something from the colored waiter, and Combe frowned because she had used the same intonation, the same facial expression, the same seductive fluidity of speech she had used when she spoke to him. "Your eggs are getting cold," he said.

What was he hoping for? Why did he suddenly want to get away from this glass cage with its blurred reflection of their dual image? Did he really expect her to go home with him, just as if they really knew one another?

She began to eat her eggs at last, with exasperatingly slow gestures. She put down her fork while she shook pepper into the glass of tomato juice she had just ordered. It was all like a slow-motion film. One of the sailors was getting sick in a corner (just as Winnie was no doubt doing at this moment). His buddy was helping him with touching concern. The waiters watched with complete indifference.

Time dragged on. An hour passed and Combe still knew nothing about this woman. He was becoming annoyed by her delaying tactics. Somehow he had got it into his mind that fate had decreed since time immemorial that she and he would leave the place together, arm in arm, and that her senseless, stubborn resistance was robbing them of the little time allotted to them.

During the hour, Combe found answers to some of the questions that had been puzzling him—her accent, for one. While her French was impeccably correct, there was a curious little intonation that showed through occasionally and that he could not define. He finally asked her if she was an American, and she replied that she had been born in Vienna.

"My name is Catherine," she said. "When I was a little girl, they called me Kathleen. Here in America they call me Kay. Have you ever been in Vienna?"

"I have."

"Oh." For the first time he noted that her expression reflected his own curiosity. After all, she knew no more about him than he did about her. It was past four in the morning. People were still coming into the lunch counter from time to time, coming from Lord knows where to haul themselves to the summit of a stool with weary sighs.

She was still eating. She had ordered a frightful-looking cake, covered with gaudy frosting, which she ate with maddening slowness, dipping the tip of her spoon into the Technicolor mess to carry away only a microscopic bit at a time. When she had finally finished, he was hopefully about to call for the check, when she ordered coffee. And as the coffee was scaldingly hot, there was more delay.

"Could you give me a cigarette? I've finished mine."

He knew that she would smoke it to the last inch, and perhaps ask for another one. He was surprised by his own impatience. What did he expect, anyhow? Once they left the counter, wouldn't she merely offer her hand and say good night?

At last they were outside. There was nobody in sight except a man who was obviously asleep, propped against the subway entrance. She did not suggest a taxi. She walked along the sidewalk, just as if the sidewalk would lead her to her chosen destination.

After they had walked about a hundred yards, during which she had stumbled a few times because of her too high heels, she hooked her hand into the crook of Combe's arm, just as though the two of them had been walking the streets of New York at five in the morning since the beginning of time.

He was to remember every detail of that night, although while he was living them they seemed so incoherent that they were not real.

Fifth Avenue stretched endlessly before them, but it was so different at this pre dawn hour that he did not recognize it until they had walked a dozen blocks and come upon a little church that he knew. Kay stopped.

"I wonder if it's open," she said. Then, with a curious touch of nostalgia in her voice, "I want so much for it to be open."

17

She made him try all the doors. They were all locked. "So it's closed." She sighed and took his arm again. A few blocks farther on she said, "My shoe hurts."

"Shall we take a taxi?"

"No, let's walk."

She had not told him her address and he had not dared ask her. It was a strange feeling to be walking like this through the vastness of the great city without the slightest idea of where they were going or what was going to happen to them in the next few hours—few minutes, even. He glimpsed their reflection in a shopwindow they were passing. Perhaps because she was tired she was leaning on him a little, and for an instant the dark image in the window was that of two lovers, a picture that only last night would have made him sick with loneliness. For the past several weeks he had found himself gritting his teeth every time he passed two people who were so obviously a couple that an aura of loving intimacy seemed to surround them. And yet here they were, he and Kay, who to the passer-by must also appear to be a couple. A funny couple, indeed.

"Would you like to drink some whisky?" she asked suddenly.

"I thought all bars were closed at this hour."

She was already in pursuit of her latest whim. She guided him around a corner into a cross street, stopped, backtracked. "No, it's not here. It's the next block. . . ."

She knocked nervously on two wrong doors before one was opened a crack by a startled man with a mop in his hand. Behind him was an empty bar and chairs stacked on tables. She cross-examined the man with a mop until she got the address she was seeking. After another fifteen minutes of trial and error, they found themselves in a basement room where three men sat at a bar, gloomily drinking.

Kay seemed to know the place. She called the barman "Jimmy." A few minutes later she remembered that his name was Teddy and went into a long explanation to the bored Ganymede. She asked about some people who had once come in with her. The bartender merely stared at her with unseeing eyes.

It took her nearly half an hour to finish her scotch, and then she wanted another one. She lit another cigarette— always the last one.

"We'll go as soon as I smoke this one," she promised.

She grew more voluble. Once outside, her grip on Combe's arm was tighter. She nearly stumbled over a curb. She spoke of her daughter. She had a daughter somewhere in Europe; where, or why the girl was not with her mother, Combe never knew.

As they reached the Forties, through the cross streets they could see the lights of Broadway paling in the coming dawn. It was nearly six o'clock. They had walked a long way and they were both weary. Combe asked suddenly, "Where do you live?"

She stopped short. At first he thought she was angry, but when he looked into her eyes—he still didn't know exactly what color they were—he saw that she was troubled, perhaps in deep distress. She dropped his arm, took several quick steps as though she was running away, then stopped again. When he had caught up with her, she looked him squarely in the eyes. Her mouth hardened as she said:

"Since this morning, I don't live anywhere."

Why was he so touched that he wanted to cry? They were standing in front of a shopwindow. His legs were so tired his knees shook; there was the bitterness of a sleepless night in his mouth and an aching emptiness in his head. Had the two whiskies done something to his nerves?

It was ridiculous. They stood there, watching each

other to see who would make the first move, both of them moist-eyed. With a stupidly sentimental gesture he seized both her hands.

"Come," he said. Then, after an instant, he added, "Come, Kay." It was the first time he had called her by name.

"Where will we go?" It was not an objection; it was a docile question.

He had no answer. He couldn't take her to his place, to that barn that he hated, to the room that hadn't been cleaned in a week, to a bed that hadn't been made.

They started walking again. Now that she had confessed she had no place to go, he was afraid of losing her. He listened. She was telling him a complicated story full of names that meant nothing to him but that she pronounced as though everybody must know them.

"I was sharing an apartment with Jessie. I wish you knew Jessie. She's the most seductive woman I've ever known. About three years ago, her husband Ronald got a very important job in Panama. Jessie tried hard to live with him down there, but her health wouldn't stand it. She had to come back to New York—with her husband's permission, of course—and we took an apartment together in the Village, not far from where you and I met. . . ."

He was listening, but he was also examining the problem of a place where they could lay their heads on the same pillow. They were still walking, although they were so tired they could neither of them feel their legs any more.

"Jessie had a lover," Kay continued, "a Chilean named Enrico. He's married, with two children, but he was about to get a divorce so he could marry Jessie. Do you follow me?"

He nodded. He was rather far behind, but he was following.

"Somebody must have written or cabled to Ronald—and I think I know who it was—so this morning Ronald arrived unexpectedly. Enrico's pajamas and bathrobe were still hanging in the closet. I had just gone out, so I missed the scene. It must have been terrible. Ronald is a man who is usually very calm, but I can imagine what he must be like when he is really furious. . . . Anyhow, when I came home at two in the afternoon, the door was locked. Our next-door neighbor heard me knocking, and gave me a letter that Jessie had left for me. I have it in my bag. . . ."

She opened her bag but couldn't look for the letter while they were crossing Sixth Avenue. Then Combe stopped under a vulgar neon-violet sign reading, "Ivy Hotel."

He nudged Kay into the lobby and spoke to the night clerk in a subdued, half-frightened voice. He finally picked up the key and its big, dangling brass disk. The clerk took them up in a tiny elevator, built for two, that smelled a little like an outhouse. Kay squeezed his arm and said in French, "Ask him to get us some whisky. I'm sure he can."

It took him several minutes to realize that she had addressed him with the familiar second-person singular, which was practically like calling him "darling."

This was the hour at which Winnie usually arose from J.K.C.'s warm love couch to tiptoe into the bathroom.

The room at the Ivy was just as drab and dusty as the daylight that had begun to filter through the drapes. Kay had dropped into a chair, thrown her fur back from her shoulders, and kicked off her black suède shoes with the too high heels. She held a glass in her hand and was sipping her drink slowly, staring into space. Her handbag was open on her lap. There was a run, like a long scar, in one stocking.

"Pour me another drink, will you, dear? It's the last one, I swear it."

She was already visibly a little giddy. She drank her whisky more quickly than usual, then sat for a moment shut up within herself, far, very far away from the room and from the man who waited without knowing exactly what he was waiting for. At last she stretched her legs—her big toes showed through the flesh pink of her stockings—and stood up.

She first turned her head away for the fraction of a second. Then very simply, so simply that the gesture might have been planned ages ago, she took two steps toward the man, threw her arms around his shoulders, raised herself on her toes, and planted her lips firmly against his.

The drone of a vacuum cleaner sounded in the hotel corridors. Downstairs the night clerk was getting ready to go home.

chapter 2

For an instant he was almost relieved to find her no longer beside him, a perplexing sentiment that a few minutes later seemed not only incredible but even shocking. Since it had not been a conscious thought, he could with almost complete honesty deny to himself that he had been guilty of disloyalty.

The room was dark when he awoke, the darkness pierced by spears of ruddy light hurled between the drapes by the neon signs in the street. He had stretched out his hand and touched only the cold sheets. Had he really been glad, had he truly and consciously believed that things would be easier and simpler if they ended thus? Apparently not, because when he saw the crack of light under the bathroom door, his heart had given a gay flip.

The sequence of events that followed left little impression on his memory; things had happened so smoothly and naturally. He had got out of bed, he remembered, because he wanted a cigarette. She must have heard him for she reached out from under the shower and opened the bathroom door.

"Do you know what time it is?" she asked gaily.

Strangely ashamed of his nakedness, he had reached for his shorts. "No, I don't know."

"Half-past seven in the evening, my dear old Frank."

Nobody had ever called him old Frank before, and the name struck a light note that vibrated in his whole being for hours. He had the marvelous feeling of being a juggler, and that life was nothing more than three or four featherweight balls to be kept in the air simultaneously. Whatever had happened before was of no importance. Nothing would matter in the future. He remembered saying, "How the devil am I going to shave?"

And she had said, with only a touch of sarcasm, "I really don't know, but if I were you, I would call room service and have a bellboy go out and get me a razor, some blades, and some shaving cream. Do you want me to call?"

She was having the time of her life. She was one of those persons who could wake up without an ache or a wrinkle, while he had not really achieved full wakefulness. For him the present was so new that it was not quite real. He remembered the most recent past—the time she had said, "You're not really fat, you know."

He replied very seriously, "I take care of myself. I'm not too old for sports." He was within an inch of flexing his muscles and swelling his chest.

The room was still strange. They had gone to bed as night was fading; they had wakened to night returning. He was afraid to leave her now, for fear that she too would disappear with the day they had not yet seen together, and that he would never find her again. Something stranger still: neither of them had thought of a good-morning kiss for the other.

She was studying the run in her stocking that he had noticed before they went to bed. She said gravely, "I must buy some stockings." She moistened her finger and applied it to the nylon scar.

He said awkwardly, "Would you lend me your comb?"

The street outside, which had been so dead when they came in, was fully awake to a noisy, glaring, blaring life—bars and restaurants side by noisy side. Their oasis of ambiguous privacy was all the more precious when they considered the carnival madness from which they were briefly isolated.

As he rang for the elevator, he asked, "Sure you've forgotten nothing?"

She nodded. They got into the elevator. A bored, gloomy girl in uniform had replaced the night man who had brought them up at dawn. In another hour the night man would doubtless be back on duty. He would have understood everything. . . .

Combe dropped his key nonchalantly on the desk while Kay went on a few steps, as poised and unconcerned as a wife or at least a mistress of long standing.

"Keeping the room?" asked the day clerk.

"Yes." Combe's affirmative was uttered quickly without thinking, partly because Kay was listening, partly because of a superstitious fear of tempting fate by trying to forecast the future.

What did he know of the future, after all? Nothing. He knew no more about Kay than she knew about him, no more than they had known on the night before, perhaps less. And yet never had two beings, two human bodies, so savagely sought mutual annihilation in fusion, so furiously shared the hunger of desperation.

25

He could not remember at which moment they had sunk into exhausted sleep. He awoke once in broad daylight. He had studied her face, still marked with unspoken sorrow, her body spread-eagled, one foot and one arm hanging over the edge of the bed. Gently he had lifted them back into place, and she had not even opened her eyes.

In the street again, they turned their back on the glaring purple sign of the Ivy Hotel. Kay took his arm again, as she had during the endless walk from the Village to the Times Square region. Now that he thought of it, he resented her having taken his arm so readily, the arm of a stranger.

"Maybe we should eat," she said with a little laugh.

"Dinner, you mean?"

She laughed outright. "Don't you think we should start with breakfast?"

He didn't know. He no longer knew who he was, how old he was, where he was. He no longer recognized the city he had crossed and crisscrossed for six months, bitterly, hopefully, tensely, hopelessly. The overwhelming power of the metropolis, its incoherence, its impersonal wonder, suddenly struck him. They were being buffeted by the street crowds as they walked, batted like ping-pong balls, and it all seemed to amuse Kay. This time it was she who was leading them, and he asked, as if it was the most natural question in the world, "Where are we going?"

"To the cafeteria in Rockefeller Center to get a bite to eat."

They threaded their way through the complex of Radio City. Kay guided them through the endless corridors of gray marble, and for the first time he was jealous. It was ridiculous, but there it was. He was jealous.

"Do you come here often?" he asked.

"Once in a while. When I'm in the neighborhood."

"With whom?"

"Idiot!"

In a single night, even less than a night, they had miraculously achieved the cycle that most lovers take weeks, sometimes months, to complete.

He was surprised to find himself eying the countermen, even the bus boys, trying to discover how well known she was in the cafeteria. If she had come there often with other men, he was sure that he would notice some sign of recognition. Why? He was not in love with Kay. He was certain that he was not in love with her. He already bristled when she fumbled in her bag for a cigarette, stained the end with her lipstick, fumbled for her lighter. He knew that she would light another as soon as she had finished the first, that she would dawdle over her coffee, and that he would want to scream when she insisted on smoking still another before beginning the agonizingly slow ritual of applying fresh lipstick while her lips pouted at the tiny mirror of her compact.

He sat through it all, nevertheless. He could not imagine any other course. He waited, resigned to this routine, resigned perhaps to many other things still to come. He caught sight of himself in a mirror across the room and recognized his smile as something from the past, a smile at once childish and tense, the smile of his college days, when he was not sure just how far some new sentimental adventure would lead him.

He was no longer a college boy. He was forty-eight years old, something he had not yet told her. They had not yet discussed the question of age. Should he tell her the truth? Or should he say that he was forty-two?

Perhaps the matter would never come up. Perhaps

they would no longer be interested in each other in another hour. Or half hour.

Perhaps that was why they had been living in slow motion since they first met, dawdling, postponing, because neither of them had as yet caught a glimpse of any possible future. . . .

They were in the street again. No doubt about it, they felt most at home in the street. Their mood changed immediately. The magic, lighthearted comradeship they had found by accident returned the moment they were again caught up in the noise and confusion of traffic.

People were lining up in front of the movie theaters. Gaudily uniformed doormen guarded the padded portals of night clubs. They passed them all by. They zigzagged aimlessly through the sidewalk crowds until she turned to him with a smile he recognized instantly. It was the smile that had started everything. He wanted to anticipate her words, to say yes before she could open her mouth. He knew what she was about to say, and, knowing that he knew, she skipped the opening question and answer.

"Just one," she said. "Shall we?"

They turned into the first bar they came to. It was a cozy little place, so made-to-order for lovers that it seemed to have been purposely placed on their path. Kay gave her companion a look that said, "You see?" Then, holding out her hand, she said, "Give me a nickel."

Without understanding, he produced the coin and she made off at once for the jukebox in the corner. She frowned as she studied the list of records with its array of shiny buttons. He had never seen her so gravely pensive. At last she found what she was looking for, pushed a button, and came back to climb on her bar stool.

"Two scotches."

A vague smile of anticipation hovered over her lips as

she listened for the first notes of her song, and for the second time he felt a pang of jealousy. With whom had she heard the tune she had sought so intently? He must have been staring stupidly at the bartender, for she said, "Listen, darling. Don't make a face like that."

The machine in the corner, after a preliminary series of clicks, had garlanded itself with a halo of orange light and began crooning in a soft, insinuating voice one of the half-whispered melodies that had been cradling the loves of thousands of Americans for the past half year or so.

She had taken his arm. She squeezed it. She smiled, and for the first time he noticed how white her teeth were; too white, perhaps; their whiteness bespoke fragility. He was about to speak, when she placed a finger across his lips and said, "Shh."

After a moment she asked, "Give me another nickel, will you?"

To listen to that same record, over and over, they were to consume considerable scotch and exchange few words.

"Doesn't this bore you?"

No, no. Nothing bored him. On the contrary, he wanted to stay with her. He had the curious feeling that he would be lost without her, and he dreaded the possibility of their separation. And yet he was in the grip of the same impatience, an almost physical sensation, that had disturbed him at the cafeteria.

The music had finally got under his skin too, with a kind of gentle, wistful tenderness, but he still wanted it to end. He told himself that when this one was finished they would go. Why must Kay interrupt their aimless wandering with such long pauses?

She asked, "What would you like to do?"

He didn't know. He had no idea what time it was. He had no desire to come down to earth, to resume the

29

routine of daily living, yet he was plagued by an indefinable uneasiness that prevented him from abandoning himself to the moment.

"What about going down to the Village? Would you mind?"

Why should he mind? He was at once very happy and very unhappy.

Outside, he saw her hesitate for an instant, and he knew why. It was surprising how each was aware of the slightest nuance of change in the other's mood. She was wondering if they would take a taxi. The question of money had never come up between them. She did not know whether he was rich or poor, and she had been startled, a moment earlier, by the size of the bar check.

He raised his arm and a yellow cab stopped at the curb on which they were standing. Like thousands and thousands of other couples at this same hour, they slid into the sweet gloom of an auto. A rainbow of bright, dancing colors whirled by each side of the driver's back.

She took off one glove and slipped her bare hand into his. They sat without speaking all the way to Washington Square. They had left the noisy anonymity of New York behind them and it was hard to believe they were in the same city. The quiet neighborhood might have been a small town anywhere in the world.

There were few people on the sidewalks and the shops were rare. A couple appeared from a side street, and it was the man who was awkwardly pushing the baby carriage.

"I'm so glad you wanted to come down here with me. I've been so happy here."

He was frightened. He wondered if she was going to tell him the story of her life. Sooner or later the time would come when she would talk about herself and he would have to talk about himself. But this was not the moment. She stopped talking. She had a way of leaning against his arm that he found tenderly charming, and now he was learning another of her gestures: she would brush her cheek against his, just a fleeting touch, so quick that he was scarcely aware of it.

"Shall we turn left here?"

They were just five minutes' walk from his place, from the room where, he suddenly remembered, he had left the light burning. He laughed to himself at the thought. She felt it. He had known her less than twenty-four hours and already he could hide nothing from her.

"Why are you laughing?"

He was about to tell her, but changed his mind at the thought she would want to see the place.

"I wasn't laughing. Not really."

She stopped at the corner of a street in which the houses were only three or four stories high. "Look," she said.

She nodded at a house with a white front. Four or five windows were lighted. "That's where I used to live with Jessie."

She nodded again, at an Italian restaurant with red-and-white-checked curtains, just beyond a Chinese laundry. "We used to eat there often, just the two of us."

She counted the windows. "There, third floor, second and third windows from the right. It's quite small, you know; just one bedroom, the living room and a bathroom."

He had been expecting to be hurt, and he was. He resented being so vulnerable and he took it out on her. His voice was almost a snarl as he demanded, "What did you do when Enrico came to see your friend Jessie?"

"I slept on the sofa in the living room."

"Always?"

"What do you mean?"

So he was right in being suspicious. She had answered a question with a question, and only after hesitating. She was obviously embarrassed.

Remembering the paper-thin wall that separated him from J.K.C. and his Winnie, he was furious. "You know very well what I mean."

"Let's walk," she said.

They walked in silence, as though they had nothing more to say to one another. Then, "Shall we go in here?"

It was a little bar, another little bar that she must know well, since it was on her street. What difference? He said yes, and regretted it immediately. This was not the cozy little bar, exciting in its intimacy, that they had left only minutes before. It was much too big, much too dreary. The bar itself was filthy, the glasses unattractive, to say the least, if not downright unsanitary.

"Two scotches," she said. "Neat." Then, "Give me a nickel anyhow."

Here too was the mechanical monster with a bellyful of records, but she couldn't find the softly confidential words of love that she was seeking. She pushed another button to kill time, while a half-tight stranger tried to barge in on their conversation.

Kay turned her back on him. They sipped their pale, lukewarm whisky.

"Let's get out of here."

When they were on the sidewalk again, she said, "You know, I've never slept with Ric."

He was about to sneer because she called him Ric instead of Enrico, but why bring that up now? She had certainly gone to bed with other men. . . .

"He did try one night—but even then, I'm not sure," she went on.

32

Why didn't she shut up? Didn't she realize that the best thing she could say at this point was nothing? Or perhaps she was torturing him deliberately. He thought of shaking off the hand that was still hooked into his arm, and walking on alone, his hands in his pockets except when he wanted to light a cigarette—or, even better, his pipe, which he had not yet flaunted before this girl.

"I don't want you to imagine things," she continued, "so I want you to know the truth. Ric is a South American, understand? One night—oh, it must have been two months ago, in August. *Tiens*, you must know how hot an August night can be in New York. Or have you ever lived through a New York August? The little apartment was like an oven. . . ."

Why was she inspiring images that he would prefer not even to entertain? He would have liked to order her to shut up. Was there no shame in a woman? Instead, he said nothing. They were walking around Washington Square. . . .

"He was beautifully built," she was saying, "but he behaved very well. He never took off his pants."

"And you?"

"What about me?"

"What did you take off?"

"I? Nothing—that I remember. I guess I was wearing my dressing gown. Jessie and I were both wearing dressing gowns."

"But you were naked under your dressing gown?"

"Probably." She didn't seem to know what he was talking about. She was so much in control of the situation that she stopped in the middle of the square to point.

"I forgot to show you Mrs. Roosevelt's hotel," she said. "That's it, over there. When he was in the White House, the President used to sneak away to spend a few days over there. He used to get away from the Secret Service even. . . ." She came back to her subject. "That night . . ."

He could have twisted her wrist to shut her up—but he didn't.

"That August night, I wanted to take a shower, so I had to go through their room. Ric had been terribly restless, I don't know why. Well, I guess I do know, now that I think back about it. He said we were all silly to act like prudes in New York in summer. He said we should all be comfortable—that we might as well take off all our clothes, the three of us, and take our shower together. Do you understand?"

"So you took your shower?" he said disdainfully.

"I took my shower—alone—and I locked the door. Ever since, I have refused to go out with him unless Jessie was along."

"But you *had* gone out with him without Jessie?"

"Yes. Why not?"

He said nothing. With the most honest air in the world, she asked, "What are you thinking about?"

"About nothing. About everything."

"Are you jealous of Ric?"

"No."

"Listen. Do you know the No. 1 Bar? No. 1 Fifth Avenue?"

He was suddenly very tired. Several times he had been so fed up with walking the streets of New York with her that he had been ready to leave her on the slightest pretext. What were they doing together anyhow, bound and riveted like two people who had always been in love and who were destined to love each other for all eternity?

Rico . . . Enrico . . . whatever his name . . . A trio for the shower. She must have been lying. He felt that she

34

was lying. He was sure of it, in fact. How could she have resisted such a mad proposal? She was lying, not to deceive him, but openly, to fill a pathological need to lie, just as she had a built-in need to ogle every man who passed, to buy with a smile the flattering glance of a bartender, a counterman, or a taxi driver. *Did you see the way he was looking at me* . . . ? She had said this about the taxi driver who had driven them from Times Square to Greenwich Village and who had probably been thinking of nothing more sexual than the size of the tip he might expect. . . .

He followed her into a room suffused with a dim, rose-tinted light. He noted an ethereal gentleman seated at a piano, nonchalantly allowing his long, pallid fingers to wander over the keyboard, releasing notes that rose like incense to fill the air with heavy nostalgia. She halted near the doorway while she told him, "Leave your coat in the checkroom."

As though he didn't know!

It was she who led the way behind the maître d'hôtel, radiant, an excited smile on her lips. She must have thought of herself as beautiful. He did not. What he found most attractive about her were the certain signs of wear in her face, the tiny lines like onionskin which at times tinged her eyelids with mauve, the occasional hints of weariness that weighed down the corners of her mouth.

"Two scotches."

She had to speak to the maître d'hôtel, to subject him to what she imagined to be her powers of seduction. With great solemnity she asked him useless questions—what numbers of the evening's show they had missed, what had become of the singer who had been there last month.

She lighted a cigarette, naturally, pushed her fur slightly away from her shoulders, tilted her head back, and sighed with pleasure. She asked:

35

"Are you unhappy?"

"Why shouldn't I be happy?"

"I don't know. But at this very minute I have a feeling that you hate me."

How sure she must be of herself to have stated the truth so simply and so bluntly! Sure of what? Why didn't he suddenly get up and go home? Why was he staying with her? To him she was neither seductive nor beautiful. She was not even young. She wore the patina of many adventures. Perhaps it was this patina that drew him to her. . . .

"Will you excuse me for a minute?"

With long, easy strides she moved to the pianist, bent over him with a smile that was once more the smile of a woman determined to charm, who would be hurt if a beggar to whom she gave a dime should refuse her a look of admiration.

She returned to the table beaming, her eyes sparkling ironically; it was for him, or at least for them, that she had used her charm this time. The pale fingers moved over the keyboard with a new rhythm now, and it was the melody of the little bar that now trembled in the rose-tinted dimness. She listened with her lips half parted, the smoke from her cigarette drifting upward past her eyes like incense.

As soon as the music had stopped, she arose, picked up her gloves, her lighter and cigarette case, and commanded, "Pay. Let's go."

As he fumbled in his pocket, she took several steps, then came back.

"You always overtip. Forty cents is plenty here." It was the final mark of possession, a take-over without argument. He did not even try to argue. Nor did he at the checkroom, where she said, "Leave her a quarter."

Outside she said, "There's no use taking a taxi."

A taxi to where? Was she so sure they were going on

together? She may have heard him telling the clerk that he would keep the room at the Ivy. Perhaps it was instinct; anyhow he was convinced that she did know. At least she asked his advice. "Shall we take the subway?"

"Not right away. I'd rather walk a little."

They were standing at the foot of Fifth Avenue, as they had the night before, and he felt a strong desire to do the same things all over again, to walk uptown beside her, to turn the same corners, perhaps even to stop at the same strange cellar where they had drunk their first whisky together. He knew that she was tired, and that walking in high heels was no fun. The idea of mild revenge, of making her suffer a little, was not displeasing to him. Besides, he wondered if she would protest. It would be a kind of experiment.

"All right. Let's walk," she said.

Had the time come for them to talk? He both hoped and feared that it was. He was in no hurry to learn more about Kay's life, but he did want to talk about his own. He wanted her particularly to know who he was, for, consciously or not, he did not enjoy being taken for just anyone, even being loved as just anyone. The night before she had not blinked an eye when he told her his name. Perhaps she had not heard clearly. Or perhaps she had not connected the name of a man she had met in a Manhattan all-night hash house with the name she must have seen in big letters on the kiosks of the Paris boulevards.

As they passed a Hungarian restaurant, she asked, "Have you ever been in Budapest?"

He said that he had, but she obviously did not care. She had gone on talking without waiting for his reply, and it was apparent that his turn had not yet come.

"What a grand city, Budapest!" she said. "I think I

was happier there than anywhere else in the world. I was sixteen."

He frowned at the word "sixteen." He was afraid another Enrico was about to rise between them.

"Mother and I were living alone. I must show you a picture of my mother. She was the handsomest woman I've ever seen."

He wondered if she might not be rambling on just to keep him from speaking. What sort of man did she think he was, anyhow? Whatever she thought, she was obviously wrong. And yet she still clung to his arm without the slightest hint of reservation.

"My mother was a very fine pianist. You must have heard her name, for she played in all the capitals of Europe. Miller, Edna Miller. That was my maiden name, and the name I took back after I was divorced. It was Mother's maiden name too. Mother would never get married on account of her art. Does that shock you?"

"Me? No." He wanted to tell her that he was not in the least shocked because he was a great artist himself. He, however, did get married, and it was on account of that . . .

He closed his eyes. When he reopened them, he saw himself as someone else might have seen him, perhaps in even sharper outline, walking up Fifth Avenue with a woman clinging to his arm, a woman he did not know and with whom he was going Lord knows where.

She continued, "Am I boring you?"

"On the contrary."

"Are you really interested in hearing about my girlhood?"

Should he try to shut her up or ask her to go on? He didn't know any more. He did know that when she spoke he felt a dull pain on the left side of his chest. Why?

Could it be because he wished that his life had begun only last night? Perhaps. But it didn't matter. Nothing mattered now, because he had suddenly decided to struggle no longer.

He listened. He walked. He studied the long line of street lights marching off into infinity. He saw the taxis go by silently, always with a couple inside. No longer did he ache to be one of a couple, to have a woman clinging to his arm.

"Let's go in here for a moment; do you mind?"

It was not a bar this time; it was a drugstore. She smiled, and he understood the smile. She felt as he did, that this marked another step in their growing intimacy: she was buying a few indispensable toilet articles.

She let him pay, and he was happy, just as he was happy to hear the clerk call her "Madam."

"Now we can go home," she said.

"Without one last scotch?" he asked ironically, and immediately regretted the tone.

"No more scotch," she announced gravely. "Tonight I'm practically a girl of sixteen. Do you mind?"

It was ridiculous that the common violet sign above the entrance to the Ivy Hotel should be a source of pleasure, like homecoming. It was ridiculous that a welcoming nod from the shabby, beaten old night clerk should be an even greater pleasure, or that he could be thrilled by the banality of a hotel room and two pillows waiting on a bed that had been turned down.

"Take off your overcoat," she said, "and sit down."

He obeyed, subtly moved. She too seemed moved. Or was she? There were moments when he hated her, and some moments, like this one, when he wanted to cry on her shoulder.

He was tired but relaxed. He waited, a faint smile on

39

his lips, a smile she caught and understood. She stooped to kiss him for the first time that day, not with the carnal hunger of their first embrace, nor with the violence born of despair. It was a gentle kiss. She advanced her lips slowly, paused at the instant of contact, then bore down tenderly. He closed his eyes. When he reopened them, he saw that she had closed hers, too. He was grateful.

"Don't move, now. Let me fix everything."

She switched out the ceiling light, leaving only the shaded lamp on the night table. Then she went to the closet for the bottle of whisky they had opened the night before.

"This isn't the same thing." She felt she had to explain.

She poured the whisky carefully into two glasses, added the water as solemnly as though she were following a recipe. She set one glass beside him, brushing his forehead with a caress as she passed.

She kicked off her shoes and curled up in a big chair like a little girl.

"Are you happy?" she asked. She sighed. Then, in a voice he had never heard before, she added, "I'm happy."

They were only a few feet apart, yet they both knew that the gap would not be closed now. They looked at each other through half-closed lids, each pleased at the responsive, peaceful glow he found in the other's eyes.

Was she about to start talking? She parted her lips, but only to sing, or rather to croon the melody that had become theirs. And the commonplace little tune became so deeply moving that tears came to his eyes and he was filled with a great warmth. She knew it, too. She knew everything. She held him to her with each note, with her warm contralto that grew husky at times. Skillfully she prolonged their pleasant awareness of being alone together, of being cut off from the world.

When she stopped, the street sounds again flowed into the silence. They listened in surprise. Then she repeated, much more softly than before, as though not to frighten destiny away, "Are you happy?"

Did he really hear her next words, or were they merely echoing inside him?

"Myself, I've never been so happy in all my life."

~~~~~~

chapter 3

It was a curious sensation. She was speaking and he was affected by what she said. But not for a single instant did he lose his lucid objectivity. He told himself, "She's lying!"

He was sure of it. Perhaps she was not making up the story—although he would not have put it beyond her—but she was certainly lying by distortion, exaggeration, or omission.

She poured herself a second drink, then a third. He knew now that this was her hour and that it was the whisky that kept her going. He could imagine her on other nights with other men, drinking to keep up her animation, talking, talking endlessly in that husky, exciting voice of hers. Did she tell them all exactly the same story with the same sincerity? He was surprised to find that he didn't care and that he did not hold it against her.

She told him about her husband, a Hungarian, Count Larski, to whom she was married when she was nineteen.

She was a virgin, she said, and went on at some length about his brutality on their wedding night. This too was a lie, or at least a half-truth; apparently she had forgotten that a little earlier she had spoken of an adventure she had had when she was seventeen. He didn't mind the lies half so much as he did the images she evoked. He didn't like her debasing herself in his eyes with a shamelessness that bordered on defiance.

Was it the whisky that made her talk this way? At one moment of cold judgment he told himself, *This is a three-o'clock woman, a woman who never wants to go to bed, who has to keep her emotions at fever pitch by any means, who must drink, smoke, and talk until from sheer nervous exhaustion she falls into the arms of a man.*

And he had not the slightest urge to run away. The more lucid he became, the more he realized that Kay was indispensable to him. And he was resigned to the fact. That was the exact word—resigned. Whatever he might find out about her in the future, he was not going to fight against the truth that he needed her.

Why didn't she stop talking? It would have been so simple. He would have put his arms around her. He would have whispered, "None of this matters, since we're starting all over again." Starting a life at zero. Two lives. Two lives at zero.

From time to time she would pause.

"You're not listening."

"Of course I'm listening."

"You're listening, but you're thinking of something else at the same time."

Yes, he was thinking of himself, of her, of everything. He was not only himself, but someone else watching himself. He could love her and still judge her implacably.

"We lived in Berlin for two years," she went on. "My

husband was attached to the Hungarian Embassy. My daughter was born in Berlin, or more exactly in Swansee on the shores of the lake. Her name is Michèle. Do you think Michèle is a pretty name?" Without waiting for an answer, she continued, "Poor Michèle! She's living with one of her aunts, a sister of Larski's who never married and who lives in a huge château a hundred kilometers from Buda. . . ."

He didn't like that huge, romantic château, although it may very well have been true. He wondered how many men she had told this story to. He scowled and she noticed it.

"Am I boring you with the story of my life?"

"Not at all."

This was something he'd have to sit through, like the last cigarette, which jangled his nerves to the finger tips. His happiness seemed to exist only in the future, and he was anxious to be done once and for all with the past and even the present. . . .

"Then he was named first secretary to Paris and we had to live at the embassy because the ambassador was a widower and he needed an official hostess. . . ."

She was lying again. Or had she been lying that night at the lunch counter, when she told him that she had lived near the Auteuil church at the corner of Rue Mirabeau. The Hungarian Embassy in Paris was never on Rue Mirabeau.

"Jean was really first-rate," she went on. "One of the most intelligent men I've ever met."

He was jealous. Why did she have to bring up another name?

"He was a great lord in his own country. You don't know Hungary—"

"Yes, I do."

"You can't. You're too French. I'm Viennese and have Hungarian blood in my veins from my grandmother's side, and even I could never get used to Hungary. When I say 'a great lord,' I don't mean one of your modern lords, but a great lord of the Middle Ages. I've seen him horsewhip his servants. Once when we were driving through the Black Forest, our chauffeur nearly turned us over. Jean made him stop the car, dragged him out, knocked him down, and stamped on his face. Then he turned to me and said calmly, 'Too bad I don't have a revolver on me. The lout might have killed you.'"

And still Combe lacked the courage to say, "For heaven's sake, shut up!"

She was belittling herself by talking and he was belittling himself by listening.

"I was pregnant at that time, which partly explains his brutal fury. He was so jealous that even a month before my baby was born he watched me from morning to night. He wouldn't let me go out alone. He locked me up in the apartment. Even better, he locked up all my shoes and clothes in one room and carried the key around with him. . . . We lived in Paris for three years. . . ."

Over bacon and eggs at 3 A.M. she had said six years. With whom had she lived the other three years?

"The ambassador died last year. He was one of our greatest statesmen. He was eighty-four years old and he took a paternal interest in me. He was a widower for thirty years and he had no children of his own."

Paternal, indeed! Not with Kay! If he had been ninety-four or even one hundred four, she would not have been happy until she had him at her feet.

"At night he would often ask me to read to him. It was one of the few pleasures left to him."

He wanted to shout vulgarly, "Where were his hands?"

but he restrained himself. He could imagine all sorts of salacious details, and the idea hurt him. He wished that she would hurry and get it all off her chest so they could forget the whole dirty business.

"Because of the ambassador, my husband claimed that the Paris air was bad for me, and we took a villa in Nogent. He got gloomier and gloomier and his jealousy went from bad to worse. Finally, I couldn't stand it any longer, and I ran away."

All alone? Come, come. If she had run away like that of her own free will, would she have abandoned her child? And if it had been she who had sued for divorce, would she be where she was now? He clenched his fists. He wanted to hit her. It would be revenge for himself and for the husband he despised.

"Is that when you went to Switzerland?" he asked, trying to suppress his sarcasm.

She caught it anyhow and she answered with sly spite.

"Not right away. First I lived on the Riviera and in Italy for a year."

She didn't say with whom she had spent the year, nor did she specify that it was alone. He hated her. He wanted to twist her arm, to force her painfully to her knees to beg forgiveness. And she had the monumental gall to sit curled up in her chair and with wide-eyed candor declare:

"You see? I'm telling everything about my whole life."

What about the things she didn't want to tell and he didn't want to hear? What about the way the old ambassador must have pawed and fondled her? He got to his feet and ordered, "Come to bed."

"May I finish my cigarette?" she asked, as he had expected.

He snatched the cigarette from her fingers, flung it to the floor, stamped it out on the rug.

"Come to bed."

She turned her head and he was sure that she was smiling triumphantly. All her talk had been cleverly designed for its cumulative aphrodisiac effect. Well, he'd show her! He wouldn't touch her tonight. Then maybe she'd understand.

Understand what? It was absurd. But then wasn't the whole adventure absurd? What the devil were two strangers doing there in a room at the Ivy, above the neon sign that winked its welcome to transient couples?

He watched without excitement as she undressed. He had no trouble remaining cold and detached. She was not the beautiful, irresistible creature that she imagined herself. Her body, like her face, wore the patina of life.

As he contemplated her supreme self-assurance, he felt an overwhelming rage rising within him. He was carried away by a mad desire to wipe out everything, consume everything, possess everything. Furiously he bore down on her, his eyes staring and vicious. She watched him stupidly, paralyzed with fright. He seized her, crushed her in his arms, swept her off her feet, plunged in deeply as though determined to root out forever the spell by which she had bewitched him. . . .

When the peace of fulfillment had succeeded the storm of the senses, Kay wept. She did not cry like Winnie would cry beyond the wall, but like a little child. And it was the voice of a little child that stammered, "You . . . you hurt me."

Still like a little child, she fell asleep without transition. This time there was no vestige of the pathetic expression that had haunted her sleep their first night together. This time she had found release. She slept soundly, her lower lip puffing slightly with each breath, both arms

48

stretched limply on the blanket, her hair an auburn tangle on the stark white of the pillow.

He did not sleep. He did not even try. Dawn was not far off, and when its first cold gray light touched the window, he arose, parted the drapes, and pressed his forehead against the coolness of the glass. The street was empty except for the trash cans lining the curb with homely expectancy. Across the street a man was shaving at a mirror hooked to the window frame. For an instant their glances met.

What had their eyes said to one another? The man was about Combe's age, balding, with thick, worried eyebrows. Was there someone behind him in the room, a woman, perhaps, still sleeping? A man who got up so early must be leaving for work. What did he do? What star guided his life?

For months, now, Combe had been following no star. But until two days ago he had at least been walking stubbornly in the same direction. On this chilly October morning, François Combe was a man without roots, a man nearing his fiftieth year, a man without ties to family, to profession, to country, to home; no ties—except to a strange woman asleep in the room of a hotel of dubious character. . . .

The light in the window across the way reminded him that he had left his light burning in the Village two nights ago. Was it an excuse he had unconsciously been seeking? Sooner or later he would have to go home. Why not now? Kay would sleep all day; he was beginning to know her habits. He would leave a note on the night table telling her that he would be back soon.

As he dressed silently in the bathroom (he had closed the door so as not to wake her), his enthusiasm grew. He would straighten up his room in the Village; he might even get someone to give it a good cleaning. He would buy some flowers. He would buy a cheap cretonne bedspread, a gaily colored print to hide his gray blanket. Then he would order dinner delivered by the Italian restaurant that served J.K.C. and Winnie every Friday. After that he would have to telephone the radio studio about a broadcast he was scheduled to make the next day. He should really have called the studio before this. . . .

Despite his fatigue he was thinking clearly and looking forward to a brisk walk alone, breathing the sharp morning air, hearing his footsteps echo on the empty sidewalks.

Kay was still sleeping soundly, puffing out her lower lip with her rhythmical breathing. He smiled a little condescendingly. She had taken a place in his life, certainly. There was no hurry to evaluate the importance of that place. If he had not been afraid of waking her, he would have kissed her gently and indulgently on the forehead.

On a blank page of his notebook he wrote, "I'll be right back." He tore out the page and slipped it under her cigarette case. That way she'd be sure to find it.

In the hallway he filled his pipe. Before lighting it he pushed the button for the elevator. The night man was off already; a girl in uniform ran the car. He went out without stopping at the desk, paused at the curb to fill his lungs. He almost sighed, "At last." He even half wondered if he would ever come back.

He walked a few steps, stopped, walked a little farther. He was suddenly worried, like a man who realizes that he has forgotten something, but can't remember exactly what. He stopped again at the corner of Broadway. The Great White Way looked very bleak without its blaze of lights. The empty sidewalks seemed unnecessarily wide. . . .

What would he do if, when he returned to the hotel, the room should be empty?

No sooner did the idea strike him than he was seized with panic. A sinking feeling gripped his entrails. He turned quickly, looking back to see if anyone was coming out of the hotel. He walked very rapidly.

At the entrance to the Ivy he knocked out his still-lighted pipe against one heel.

"Eighth floor, please," he told the girl who had just brought him down.

His heart pounded as he slipped the key into the lock. Kay was still asleep. He took a deep breath.

He didn't know if she had seen him go out or come in. She seemed to be still asleep while he undressed. She didn't budge when he slid back into bed. Even when she snuggled against him, he could have sworn she was asleep.

She did not open her eyes, but her eyelids fluttered faintly like the wings of a bird learning to fly. Her lips moved. Her voice seemed to come from far away as she murmured, without a note of reproach, of sadness, or the slightest trace of melancholy, "You tried to run away, didn't you, darling?"

He almost answered her, and he would have spoiled everything. Luckily for him, she continued in the same voice, farther away than ever, "But you couldn't do it!"

She was asleep again. Perhaps she had not really wakened, but was speaking from the depths of some dream. When they awoke together hours later, she made no reference to his absence or to her remark.

It was their most delightful hour. It was impossible to believe that this was only the second time they had awakened together in the same bed. The warm intimacy of flesh to flesh was so familiar they felt as though they had always been lovers and that there had been thousands of mornings like this. Even the drab bedroom of the Ivy was part of that familiarity.

51

"Do I get the bathroom first?" she asked. Then, with surprising perceptivity, "Why don't you smoke your pipe? I don't mind, darling. In Hungary, lots of women smoke pipes."

They were both very gay. There was something virginal, almost childish about their eyes on awakening. They were playing at life.

"When I think of all the things that I'll probably never see again because of Ronald. I have two trunks full of clothes and lingerie down there. And here I can't even change my stockings."

She laughed about it. Standing at the threshold of a new day, without worrying about what was to go into it, generated a marvelous feeling.

The sun was shining when they went out, a laughing, sparkling sun, and they decided to have breakfast at a lunch counter not unlike the one in which they had first met.

"Shall we go for a walk in Central Park?"

"Why not?" he said. He tried not to be jealous so early in the day, yet every time she mentioned another place, he wondered with whom she had been there before. What memories would she find in Central Park?

She looked young this morning. Perhaps it was because she also felt young that she said solemnly, as they walked into the park, "Do you know that I'm already quite an old woman, darling? I'm thirty-two. I'll soon be thirty-three."

He calculated that her daughter must be about twelve, and he paid closer attention to the girls playing in the park.

"I'm forty-eight," he confessed. "Well, not quite. But I will be in another month."

"Men have no age."

Perhaps this was the moment to talk about himself. He hoped so. And he dreaded it, too.

What would happen when they finally decided to look reality in the face? Up to this moment they had been skirting the fringes of life, but the time must come when they would have to crash into the heart of the matter. Was she reading his mind, as usual? Her bare hand sought his, as it had once before, in the taxi. She squeezed gently but insistently as if to say, "Not yet."

He had made up his mind to take her home—if that was the word—to his cell in the Village, but he didn't dare —yet. She had not noticed that he had paid the bill at the Ivy when they left, and he had not mentioned it to her. That might mean many things, including, among others, the possibility that this would be their last walk together. In any case, it would be their last before they re-entered reality. Perhaps that was the reason she had suggested this stroll, arm in arm, in Central Park, where the last warmth of an autumn sun might bless them with a friendly smile.

She was humming as she walked—the silly little tune of the jukebox which had become their song. Her muted notes gave them both the same idea. The shadows were lengthening, the sun was swinging low over the towers of Central Park West, the wind was beginning to bite. By tacit, mutual agreement, they turned their steps toward Fifth Avenue.

He didn't hail a taxi. They walked, as though that was to be their destiny for all time—walking up or down Fifth Avenue, elbowing through crowds that were not there or were without their consciousness. The moment was approaching when they would have to stop walking—and by tacit agreement, they were postponing it indefinitely.

"Listen . . ." There were times when, by the whole posture of her body, she could express a kind of naïve joy.

This happened instinctively when she felt that Fate was on her side—as when they walked into a little bar and the jukebox was playing their song, and there was a homesick sailor, in contrast, leaning his elbows on the bar and staring into space. Kay squeezed Combe's arm and favored with a compassionate glance the man who had chosen her favorite melody to nurse his nostalgia.

"Give me a nickel," she whispered.

She borrowed a second nickel, a third. The sailor turned his head and gave her a sad smile. Then he gulped his drink and staggered out, bumping into the doorjamb on the way.

"Poor guy!" she said.

He was almost jealous; maybe he was, just a little. He wanted to talk about himself; he wanted desperately to talk about himself, and still he could not overcome the block. What's more, she wasn't helping him. Was she doing this purposely?

She was drinking again. He didn't mind. He was matching her, drink for drink, mechanically. He was happy, and he was depressed. His emotions were so close to the surface that his eyes dimmed at a single phrase from the jukebox or a sentimental movement in the romantic half-light of the lounge.

They moved on. They walked on Broadway tonight. They pushed through the crowds and entered bar after bar —none of them as intimate as *their* bar. But the routine was the same.

"Two scotches."

Then Kay would light a cigarette, nudge him, and whisper, "Look."

And she would nod at a couple obviously lost in unhappy thoughts, or a lonely woman seriously embarked on a roaring drunk. She seemed to be stalking the despair of

54

others in the hope that the contact would immunize her against the virus that she herself had been fleeing.

"Let's go." They looked at each other and smiled. It was a password they knew well—even though their intimacy had spanned only two nights. "It's funny, isn't it?" she added.

He didn't have to ask her what was funny. They were thinking of the same thing, although they were little more than strangers who had met by some selective miracle in the world's biggest city and now clung to one another as if the cold of loneliness was about to close in on them again.

Combe thought, *Soon . . . a little later.*

There was a Chinese shop on Forty-second Street that advertised "Baby Turtles."

"Buy me one, will you, darling?"

They put it into a little cardboard box that Kay carried very carefully—and laughingly—for it was the only pledge of love that he had offered her.

"Listen, Kay."

She stroked his lips with her finger, meaning silence.

"But Kay, I must tell you . . ."

"Not now. Let's get something to eat."

They dawdled deliberately, because now they knew definitely that they were really at home only in the street crowds of New York.

They ducked into a lunch counter, and again they dawdled. She ate with an exasperating slowness that no longer exasperated him. She said:

"There are so many more things that I want you to know, my darling. You see, I know what you think, and you are so wrong, my Frank."

They were walking again. It was Fifth Avenue again, but in the other direction. Twice they had made the long trek uptown; tonight they were walking downtown.

"Where are you taking me?" She thought better of her question, and added, "No, don't tell me."

He wasn't sure what he was going to do or even what he wanted to do. He stared straight ahead as he walked, and she, for once, respected his silence. After a while this silent promenade down Fifth Avenue became so solemn that it struck them both as a bridal march. They edged closer together, not as lovers, but as two creatures who had been wandering blindly in the fog of solitude and who had finally been granted the unexpected favor of a human contact. For the moment they were scarcely aware of being male and female. They were two human beings, two beings who needed one another.

They were dead tired by the time they reached the tranquil surroundings of Washington Square. Combe knew that his companion must be wondering if he might not be taking her back to the lunch counter that was the fountainhead of their relationship, or perhaps to the house where Jessie lived, the house she had pointed out the night before.

He smiled to himself, a little bitterly, because he was afraid, very much afraid, of what he was going to do. He had never told her that he loved her, nor had she told him that she loved him. Why not? Superstition? Fear of the word *love?* Reserve?

Not far ahead Combe could see the house he had fled only forty-eight hours before, rather than submit to another night of torture by the love cries of his neighbors. Tonight he was walking right back into the torture chamber, solemnly erect because he was about to accomplish an act of great importance.

Once or twice he was on the point of turning back, of dragging Kay back into the unreality of their vagabond days. He closed his eyes and saw as a safe harbor the flashing neon sign of the Ivy, the down-at-the-heel night clerk, the bed that was their bed. . . . It would be so much easier.

He stopped at the entrance of the building he reluctantly called home. "Come," he said.

She did not underestimate the importance of the occasion. She realized that the moment was as solemn as if a resplendent Swiss guard had thrown open the portals of the church. She crossed the little courtyard valiantly, surveying the surroundings quietly and without surprise.

"How funny!" she said in her gayest voice. "Here we've been neighbors all along, and yet we didn't meet for ages."

They crossed the little lobby with its wall panel of names and buttons. Combe's name was not there, and he saw that she had noticed this.

"Come," he said. "There's no elevator."

"It's only four stories," she said. She must have counted from the street.

She climbed the stairs ahead of him. On the third landing she stepped aside to let him pass. The first door to the left was J.K.C.'s; the next was his. Before moving on, however, he looked at the woman for a long moment. Then he took her into his arms and pressed a long, slow kiss upon her lips.

"Come."

The dimly lit hallway smelled of poverty. Grimy fingers had smudged the walls. Standing in front of the ugly brown door, he drew his key slowly from his pocket. Forcing a laugh, he said:

"The last time I went out I forgot to turn off the light. I noticed it from the street but I didn't have the courage to climb back up the stairs."

He pushed open the door. The tiny foyer was cluttered with trunks and clothing.

"Come in," he said. He didn't dare look at her. He said nothing. With trembling fingers he took her hand, drew her inside, and, anxious and half ashamed, pushed her gently into his life.

There was something unreal about the quiet of the room. He had expected that the lighted lamp would reveal a scene that was sordid; instead he saw only the tragic—the forlorn tragedy of loneliness: the unmade bed with the rumpled sheets that spelled insomnia; the dented pillow that still held the shape of his head; his slippers lying where he had kicked them off; his pajamas and a soiled shirt thrown over the back of a chair; on the table an open book beside a paper plate on which lay a half-eaten sandwich, the sorry meal of a man alone.

He suddenly realized what he had escaped, even briefly, and he stood motionless in the foyer, not daring to speak. He didn't want to look at her, but he couldn't help noticing that she too was struck by the great depth of his loneliness. He had thought that she would be surprised and resentful. She was not resentful, although she may have been just a little surprised that his solitude had been even more complete than hers.

The first things she saw were the photographs of two children, a boy and a girl. She murmured, "You too?"

It all went so slowly, exasperatingly slowly, that every second counted, each tenth of a second, the tiniest fraction of time enfolded so much of the past—and of the future.

Combe turned away from the photos of his children, which had become blurs and were growing even more indistinct. He was ashamed of himself and wanted to ask someone's pardon, whose or why he didn't know.

Kay slowly crushed out her cigarette in an ash tray. She stepped behind Combe to close the door he had left open. Then, touching him lightly between the shoulders, she said:

"Take off your overcoat, darling."

It was she who helped him off with it, and she knew exactly where to hang it in the closet. When she turned to face him again, she seemed very human, very much at home. She smiled as though nurturing some secret joy that she was not quite ready to confess. As she wound her arms around him at last, she said, "You see, darling, I've known it always."

chapter 4

~~~~~~

They slept that night as in a railway-station waiting room,
or in a stalled auto by the roadside. They slept in each
other's arms but they did not make love.

"Not tonight," she had whispered prayerfully.

He had understood, or at least thought he did. They
were both bone-tired and suffering from the sort of dizziness
that is often the aftermath of a long voyage. Had they actually arrived somewhere? They had gone to bed at once,
without touching the disorder of the room. And, like trav-
elers home from the sea who feel the pitch and roll of the
ship for the first few nights, they felt the impact of the great
city's pavements in their legs that night as in their dreams
they walked endlessly up and down Fifth Avenue.

For the first time they arose at the same hour as other
people. When Combe opened his eyes, he saw Kay opening the door into the hallway. Perhaps the click of the latch
had awakened him. He was startled, puzzled. She had her

back to him. At first he was aware only of the silken tangle of her hair. Then he saw that she was wearing one of his dressing gowns and that it dragged on the floor.

"What are you looking for?"

She didn't jump. She turned naturally toward the bed without a smile. She said:

"The milk. Don't you have milk delivered every morning?"

"I never drink milk."

"Oh." She stepped into the kitchenette, where a kettle was singing on the electric hot plate. "Do you drink tea or coffee?"

It was exciting to hear her familiar voice in this cubicle, which had never, during his occupancy, had a visitor. An instant earlier he had been a little put out because she had not kissed him good morning. But it was much better that she find her way around, making herself at home by daylight, opening drawers and closets. She brought him a navy-blue silk dressing gown.

"Is this one all right?"

She was lost in his bedroom slippers, and the heels slapped the floor as she walked.

"What do you usually eat for breakfast?"

"That depends." He leaned back, relaxed. "When I'm very hungry, I go down to the drugstore."

"I found some tea and a can of coffee. Since you're French, I took a chance and started the coffee."

"I'll go downstairs for the bread and butter." He was feeling very young. He was anxious to get out, but it wouldn't be like yesterday, when he had been unable to go more than a hundred yards from the Ivy. Today she was here, in his apartment. Today he was tempted to go out in bedroom slippers without even shaving, the way Parisians did in Montmartre or Montparnasse, but the well-groomed François Combe could not quite stoop to this.

There was spring in the air that autumn morning, and he hummed in his shower while she made the bed. She too was humming. He felt as though a great weight of years had slipped from his shoulders, a weight he had never been conscious of but that had nonetheless made him stoop.

"Aren't you going to kiss me?"

She gave him the ends of her lips before he closed the door. He started down the stairs, then came back. When he opened the door again she was still standing there.

"Kay!"

"What?"

"I'm happy."

"So am I. Go on . . ."

He ran down the stairs two at a time. He mustn't let down now. It was all so new. Even the street was different. The drugstore, for instance, where he had so often eaten his solitary breakfast while reading the paper, now seemed an object to be regarded with joyous irony, tinged with pity. He stopped to watch an organ-grinder playing his heart out at the curb—the first he had ever seen in New York, the first, in fact, he had seen since he was a boy. The Italian food shop was new too. He used to buy only for one, but today he ordered a dozen little things he had never wanted before but now seemed essential to stock the refrigerator.

He took the bread and butter, the milk and the eggs with him and had the rest delivered. On his way out he remembered something and came back.

"Please leave a quart of milk at my door every morning."

Kay was at the window as he came down the street and she waved to him. She met him at the head of the stairs to take some of his packages.

"*Zut!*" he said. "I forgot something."

"What?"

"The flowers. Since yesterday morning I've been planning to put flowers in the room."

"Don't you think it's better this way?"

"Why?"

"Because . . ." She groped for words, smiling but still serious. They were both a little bashful this morning. "Because it doesn't seem so new this way. I'd rather feel like this has been going on for a long time." Then, as though to avoid getting sentimental, she added quickly, "Do you know what I was looking at when you saw me at the window? I was watching an old Jewish tailor just across the street. Haven't you ever noticed him?"

He vaguely remembered seeing an old man sitting cross-legged on a table in a window opposite. He had a long, untidy beard, and the fingers that plied the needle all day long had seemed unhygienically dark.

"When I was living in Vienna with my mother—I told you, didn't I, that my mother was a famous concert pianist? Well, she was. But before she got to be famous, she had a hard time. When I was little, we lived in one room. . . . Oh, not nearly as nice as this! There was no kitchenette, no bathroom, and no refrigerator. There wasn't even any running water, and we had to use the tap at the end of the hall to wash ourselves, like the rest of the tenants. If you only knew how cold it was in winter. . . .

"What was I saying? Oh yes . . . When I was sick—I used to get the grippe—and had to stay home from school, I used to look out the window all day, when they didn't keep me in bed. And right across the street there was an old Jewish tailor just like this one, and when I looked out a little while ago and saw *this* man, I thought for a moment he was the same tailor."

"Maybe he is." Combe was teasing.

"Idiot! He would be at least a hundred years old. But don't you think it's a curious coincidence? It put me in good humor for the rest of the day."

"Did you need that?"

"No . . . but I still feel like a little girl today, and when I was young, I liked to make fun of people. I even feel like making fun of you."

"What have I done now that's ridiculous?"

"Do you mind if I ask you a question?"

"I'm listening."

"How does it happen that there are at least eight dressing gowns in your closet? Maybe I shouldn't ask a question like that, but I must say that it's rather unusual for a man—"

"For a man who has so many dressing gowns to live in a Village dump like this? Is that your question? Well, the answer is quite simple. I'm an actor."

Why had he dropped those words so modestly, while avoiding her eyes? Why were they so careful of each other's sensibilities this morning, as they faced each other across the breakfast table (not yet cleared), and across the street from the old tailor with the rabbinical beard?

This was the first time, really, that they had been face to face without the supporting anonymity of the faceless New York street crowds, without the stimulus of scotch or a jukebox singer. They were, in a way, seeing each other for the first time. Kay had put on no lipstick—which gave her a new face—gentler, sweeter, with a touch of timidity; perhaps a little fearful. The change was striking. The eternal cigarette didn't quite fit the new Kay.

"Are you disappointed?" he asked.

"That you're an actor? Why should I be disappointed?" But she said it a little sadly, and because they understood each other without words, they both knew that this was serious. If he were an actor, and at his age had come down to a one-room kitchenette apartment in Greenwich Village . . .

"It's much more complicated than you think," he sighed.

"But I wasn't thinking of anything, *mon chéri*."

"I was quite well known in Paris. I might even say that I was famous."

"I must admit that I don't remember your name. I know you told me, but only once, that night I first met you. Do you remember? I was so upset that I didn't dare ask you to repeat it."

"François Combe. I used to play at the Théâtre de la Madeleine, at the Michodière, at the Gymnase. I've toured all Europe and South America. I have been the star of many films. Only eight months ago, I was offered an important contract. . . ."

He watched her for some sign of pity that would have hurt him deeply. There was none.

"You are probably jumping to wrong conclusions," he said. "Any time I want to go home, a dozen producers will be after me with contracts."

She poured him a fresh cup of coffee and he looked at her in surprise. It was such a natural gesture he could not believe that this homely, familial intimacy that had crept upon them unsuspected could be less than miraculous.

"It was very simple and very stupid," he said. "It's no secret. It was the talk of Paris. The newspaper columnists had a field day. My wife is also an actress—quite a fine actress, in fact: Marie Clairois . . ."

"I know the name." She was obviously sorry that she she had pronounced those words, but it was too late. The fact that she had recognized his wife's professional name but not his was now a matter of record.

"She's not much younger than I am," he went on. "She's on my side of forty. She was seventeen when I married her. Our son will soon be sixteen."

He spoke without passion, although he was looking at the photographs on the wall. He got up and began pacing as he continued:

"Last winter my wife abruptly announced that she was leaving me to live with a young actor who had just been engaged by the Théâtre-Français. He had just been graduated by the Conservatoire. He was twenty-one years old. I remember the night. I had just come home from the theater. She was not home yet. It was in our house at Saint-Cloud, a house I had built myself because I like houses. My tastes are rather bourgeois, you know.

"I was in the library when she came home. She announced her decision with poise, much kindness, quite a bit of affection, and I might say even tenderness. I had no way of knowing, of course, that the young upstart was waiting outside in a taxi, ready to carry her off as soon as she had finished her chore of making a clean breast to her husband. I must confess—"

He stopped and cleared his throat, suddenly aware that he was making an impersonal declaration, quite unsuitable to his present audience.

"I must confess, darling," he resumed, "that I was so stunned, so dumfounded, that I asked her to think it over. I can see now how ridiculous I must have sounded when I said, 'Go to bed, my girl. We'll talk this over tomorrow when you've had a chance to sleep on it.'

"She said, 'But François, I'm leaving you right this minute. Can't you understand?'

"What didn't I understand? Why she was in such a

hurry that she couldn't wait until morning? I didn't understand, that much was true. I think today I might have understood. But that night I lost my temper. I must have said some pretty awful things to her.

"She never lost her quiet, patient manner, however. She was sweet and, I suppose, a little maternal. She repeated, over and over, 'What a pity, François, that you cannot understand!'"

He stopped, and the silence was so tenuous, so delicate, that it was neither embarrassing nor distressing. He lighted his pipe with a self-assured gesture that he had used in several of his favorite stage roles.

"I don't know whether you've ever seen Marie in the theater or on the screen," he continued. "She still plays young heroines, and she can still get away with it. She has a very sweet face, sensitive and a little sad, with big, innocent eyes that look out at you with such candor that— Well, like the eyes of a wounded fawn that can't believe the wicked hunter with the gun could possibly have meant any harm. That was the kind of part she always played, on the stage and in real life, and that was the part she was playing that night.

"Every paper in Paris told the story, some by insinuation, others cynically. The kid threw away the prestige of the Comédie-Française to join my wife in a new play opening on the *boulevards*. The Comédie sued him for breach of contract. . . ."

"And your children?"

"The boy is in England. He's been at Eton for two years and I thought he ought to stay there. My daughter is living in the country with my mother, near Poitiers. I stayed there myself for two months. I suppose I could have stayed on."

"Did you love her?"

He stared at Kay, uncomprehending. For the first time since they had met, words meant different things to each of them.

"They offered me a part in an important film, a starring part. She was in it too, and I was sure that she would somehow get her lover a part as well. We can't get away from each other, in our business. For instance, since we lived in Saint-Cloud, and we drove home separately after our separate performances, we would frequently meet at Fouquet's on the Champs-Elysées. . . ."

"I know Fouquet's."

"Like most actors I know, I never used to eat before a performance, but I would have a hearty supper afterward. I had my own table at Fouquet's and they knew exactly what to serve me. Well, believe it or not, only a few days after my wife's dramatic farewell, she turned up at Fouquet's after the theater. And she wasn't alone, either. She came to my table and greeted me so simply, so naturally, that I had the curious feeling that the two of us—the three of us, rather—were playing a scene from something by Sacha Guitry.

"She said, 'Bonsoir, François.' The young interloper held out his hand, too, and stammered, 'B-bonsoir, Monsieur Combe.' I knew they expected me to invite them to sit at my table, and with fifty people watching breathlessly, could I afford to be ungracious? What's more, my supper was already being served.

"I saw there were several newspapermen in my audience, but I am not sure I realized the full consequences of my words when I announced, loudly enough for the audience to hear:

"'I think I'll be leaving Paris shortly.'

"'Where are you going?' my wife asked.

" 'I've been offered a contract in Hollywood, and now that there's nothing to keep me here . . .'

"Cynicism? Indifference? No. I don't believe she was very cynical. She believed what I said. She knew very well that I had received an offer from Hollywood four years before, and that I had turned it down, partly because she had not been included in the deal, and partly because I did not want to be separated from the children.

"She said to me, 'I'm very happy for you, François. I have always been sure that everything would work out.'

"I had left them standing in front of my table until that moment. Then I asked them to sit down—why, I still don't know.

" 'What may I offer you?'

" 'You know very well that I never eat supper, François. I'll have some fruit juice.'

" 'And you, young man?'

"The imbecile was in great need of a drink to restore his poise, but he thought it his duty to follow the lead of his mistress. He said, 'Two fruit juices, Maître d'Hôtel.'

"The two of them sat watching me while I ate my supper. My wife took her compact from her bag and asked, 'Have you heard from Pierrot?' Pierrot was our boy's nickname. 'I had a letter three days ago,' I said. 'He's still quite happy there.' 'So much the better,' my wife said.

"Believe it or not, Kay—"

Why she chose that exact moment to interrupt he never knew. She said, "Don't you want to call me Catherine?"

He reached out for her hand and squeezed it.

"Believe it or not, Catherine, all during my supper, my wife sat there giving encouraging glances to that young fool, as though to say, 'See how simple it is? There was no reason to be frightened.' "

"You still love her, don't you?" Catherine said.

He frowned. He got up and walked around the room twice, pausing at the window to stare at the old Jewish tailor across the way. Then he planted himself in front of her, his head turned slightly so that the light would flatter his profile. He paused an instant, as he did on the stage to give full effect to a particularly dramatic line he was about to deliver.

"No!"

He wanted no scene. He himself felt no emotion, and he was particularly anxious that Kay should not misinterpret his feelings. He began talking rapidly, sharply.

"I left Paris for the United States. A friend of mine, one of our top directors, had once said to me, 'There's always a spot for you in Hollywood. A man of your talent and reputation doesn't have to wait for a contract. Go on out there. Go to see So-and-so. Or So-and-so. Tell them I sent you.'

"I went. Everyone was very polite. They welcomed me with open arms—and not a single job offer. One producer said, 'We're considering a story that has a fat part in it for you. If we decide to make the picture, we'll let you know.' Another one said, 'We'll have our production schedule set up in a month or so. Keep in touch.' So you see, Kay—"

"I asked you to call me Catherine."

"Forgive me. I'll get used to it. Some of my best Parisian friends were working in Hollywood. They were wonderful. They did their best to help me, but I turned out to be a dead weight. Rather than upset their busy lives, I came to New York. Contracts are signed just as easily here as in California.

"At first I lived in a swank Park Avenue hotel. Then I moved to a more modest hotel. And finally I found this place. For six months I've lived in New York alone. That's the whole story. Alone. Now you know why I have so many dressing gowns, so many suits, so many pairs of shoes."

His voice broke a little. He turned again to the window, pressed his forehead against the pane. He knew that she would come to him, silently, sympathetically. He expected the gentle touch of her hand on his shoulder. He didn't move. He stared at the bearded tailor across the street, smoking a porcelain pipe.

A voice whispered in his ear, "Are you still very unhappy?"

He shook his head negatively, but he wouldn't, couldn't face her yet.

"Are you sure that you don't love her any more?"

At that, he lost his temper. He spun about, his eyes blazing.

"You idiot! Haven't you understood a word I've said?" Yet she must understand. It was too important, the most important thing in the world. And if she couldn't understand, who else could? It was so easy to follow the line of least resistance, to blame everything on a woman.

He placed the floor feverishly, so angry that he refused to look at her.

"Can't you see that my wife doesn't matter, that I'm the only one that counts? I . . . ! I . . . !" He almost screamed the word. "I, alone, if you like. I, who found myself stripped naked before the world! I, who lived here alone, yes, for half a year, alone! And if you can't understand that, you . . . you . . ."

He stopped himself before he shouted, "You aren't worthy of being here yourself." He lapsed into silence, like a brat exhausted by a silly temper tantrum.

He wondered what Kay was thinking, whether her expression showed her reaction, but he stubbornly refused to look at her. He stood with his hands in his pockets, staring

72

at the wall. Why didn't she help him? Wasn't this the time for her to make the first move? Did she really think that all his trouble arose from stupid sentimentality? Did she imagine that his suffering was that of a common cuckold? She made him sick. He was prepared to hate her all over again. He leaned his head to one side. When he was a small boy, his mother used to say that she could tell when he was slyly plotting mischief because he would lean his head toward his left shoulder.

He stole a glance at Kay with only one eye. She was smiling and crying, both at once. Although there were tears on her cheeks, there was happy compassion in her face, as if she was not sure which expression she should adopt.

"Come here, François."

She was too intelligent not to realize what she was risking by summoning him at a moment like this. Was she that sure of herself?

"Come here." She spoke to him as if she addressed a stubborn child. "Come."

He took a reluctant step toward her. She should have been a ridiculous figure in that borrowed dressing gown that swept the floor, the slippers that dropped off her little feet each time she moved, her face free of make-up, her hair still sleep-tangled. But she wasn't. She drew him toward her as by some tropism. All he could do was look surly.

"Come." She took his head between her hands, pressed it against her cheek. She did not kiss him. She held him close, so that her warmth would gradually make him aware of her presence. He did not melt easily; that last trace of bitterness was hard to give up.

Then she whispered, so softly that he would not have heard the words had not her lips been against his ear, "You were not so lonely as I was."

73

Did she feel him stiffen a little? She was sure of herself, however, or perhaps sure of their mutual loneliness that would forever make it impossible for one to dispense with the other.

"There's something I must tell you, too." It was still a whisper, and, what was stranger still, a whisper in broad daylight, without muted incidental music, without any background more romantic than a window framing an untidily bearded, cross-legged old tailor sewing quietly across the way.

"I know that I'm going to hurt you," she said, "because you are jealous. I'm glad that you're jealous. But I have to tell you this anyhow. When we first met—"

She didn't say, "day before yesterday," and he was grateful to her for the omission. He did not like to remember that they had known each other for so short a time.

"When we first met . . ." Her voice was so low now he felt her words vibrating against his chest, rather than heard them. ". . . I was so alone, so hopelessly alone, so darkly depressed that I was sure that I could never climb out to daylight again, that I had decided to go home with the first man who asked me, any man . . ." She paused. Then, "François, I love you."

She said it only once. She could not have repeated it anyhow, because she was so tightly locked in his arms that speech was impossible. Their embrace was so tight that everything seemed to stop—their breathing, perhaps even their heartbeats. What could either of them say after that? What could they have done? They could not even have made love. That would have ruined everything.

The man did not dare relax his embrace. They were so close now that any relaxation might have produced a fatal vacuum. It was she who freed herself, gently, simply, and smilingly. She said:

74

"Look across the street." As he turned his head, she added, "He saw us."

A sunbeam slanted across their window and seemed to focus deliberately on the wall, a few inches from the photographs of his two children.

"François," she said, "you'll have to go out for a while."

While there was still sunlight in the streets, sunlight in the city, sunlight in his heart. She knew that he would have to go out now, to get his feet on the ground, to re-establish contact with reality. It was essential for him—for them.

"I want you to change your clothes," she went on. "Yes, I insist. I'll pick the suit I want you to wear."

There were so many things he wanted to tell her, after the confession she had just made. Why had she changed the subject? She had thrown open the closet and was fingering his suits, quite at home, humming to herself—and to him. It was their song, and she began to sing it as she had never sung it before, with a contralto that was at once solemn and gay, a voice that transformed the banal refrain into the quintessence of all they had just lived through.

She was still going through the wardrobe, switching from a song to a monologue: "No, monsieur. No gray today. No beige, either. Beige is not becoming to you, whatever you may think. You're neither dark enough nor fair enough to wear beige." She laughed. "By the way, what color is your hair? I've never noticed. Your eyes, yes. Your eyes change color to fit your moods. A few minutes ago, when you were resigned to playing the role of victim—or almost resigned—your eyes were an ugly dark gray, like a heavy sea that makes all passengers seasick. I was wondering if you would be able to make the last few yards to shore, or whether I would have to come to your rescue.

"All right, *monsieur*. Mind Mamma, François. It will be navy blue. You will be magnificent in navy blue."

He wanted to give her an argument, but he lacked the energy. Why, at this moment, was he again thinking, *She is not even beautiful?* And why had he not returned the compliment and told her that he loved her, too? He wished he had.

Perhaps he didn't love her, or at least was not sure. He needed her—that *was* sure—and he had a terrible fear of losing her and finding himself once more alone. As to what she had just confessed—he was grateful to her for being frank, and furious at her for what she might have done. Suppose it had been somebody else instead?

Condescending yet moved, he let her dress him as though he were a schoolboy. He knew that she wanted no more serious declarations, no more grave pronouncements that morning. He knew that she was playing at being a wife, a very difficult role to play if there is no love.

"I'll wager, Mr. Frenchman, that you always wear a bow tie with this suit. Very well, to make you look even more French, I'm going to choose a blue bow with white polka dots."

She was so right that he had to smile, even though he felt a little sheepish. He didn't want to appear ridiculous.

"And a white handkerchief for your breast pocket, right? Just a trifle mussed so you won't look like a store-window dummy. Where do you keep your handkerchiefs?"

It was silly. It was so idiotic. They laughed together. They were acting, both of them, with tears in their eyes, pretending they were not being softies.

"I'm sure you have people to see," she said. "Now don't deny it. Don't lie to me. I insist that you see them."

"Well, there's the radio studio . . ."

"Then you're going to the studio. When you're

through, come home. I'll be here." She felt that he was afraid. She was so sure of it that she sealed her promise by squeezing both his arms very hard. "All right, François. *Hinaus!*" She had never used a German word before. She reverted immediately to French. "*Filez, monsieur.* And don't expect to find an elaborate luncheon when you come home." They were both thinking of Fouquet's, but neither would have admitted it. "And you must wear a topcoat. This one. And a black hat. Yes, I insist."

She eased him toward the door. She had not yet had time to wash her face or comb her hair. He knew that she wanted to be alone, and he was not sure whether he should be angry or grateful.

"I'll give you two hours," she said. "Three at most." She closed the door after him, but opened it almost immediately. She was obviously embarrassed. "François!"

He came back up the few stairs.

"Forgive me for asking," she said, "but could you let me have a few dollars to get things for lunch?"

He blushed. Why had he not thought of this himself? He fished his wallet from his pocket. He had never felt more embarrassed in his life. Standing by the door with the green initials J.K.C., he drew out several bills—ones, fives, he didn't count them. He blushed even deeper.

"I'm sorry," she said.

He knew. So was he. The question of money had never before come up between them. He wanted to go back into the apartment and tell her what was on his mind, but that would only make matters worse.

"Do you mind if I buy a pair of stockings?"

He understood, or thought he did, that this was a deliberate question, designed to restore his self-confidence, to restore him to his role of master of the house.

"Forgive me for not having thought of it," he said.

"You know, I may be able to get back my baggage yet." She was still smiling. All this had to be done with a smile, with the very special smile that had seen them through that morning. "But don't worry. I won't spend it all on furs, darling."

He looked at her. She was still without make-up, had no concern for the strange picture sketched by the too long dressing gown and the too big slippers that were forever escaping her.

He stood two steps below the landing.

He climbed them at once.

There, in the anonymous no man's land of the dingy hallway, they exchanged their first real kiss of the day, perhaps the first real kiss of their acknowledged love. And they were both so much aware of all it implied, all the things it promised, that they prolonged the sweetness of its tender pledge until the sound of a door closing somewhere brought them back to reality. Their lips parted at last. She said simply:

"Go."

As he went down the stairs, he felt like a new man.

~~~~~~

chapter 5

François Combe's New York career had not been exactly brilliant. He had played the part of a Frenchman in a show that survived a Boston tryout but died after three weeks on Broadway. A French playwright named Laugier, who had been living in New York for two years, got him an occasional radio job.

This morning he felt no bitterness about his dismal American experiences. He walked to Washington Square to take a Fifth Avenue bus. The avenue was bathed in sunlight, giving the gray buildings a golden patina that was almost transparent at times. The sky was a pristine blue except for an occasional fluffy cloud like those which artists paint around saints and angels.

He was still lighthearted when he got off the bus but as he walked toward the radio studio, he began to feel a vague uneasiness, perhaps a foreboding.

A foreboding of what? The thought crossed his mind that when he got home Kay would no longer be there. He shrugged it off. He watched himself do the actual shrugging, for he had stopped in front of an art dealer's window and could see his reflection. Why did this uneasiness grow on him the farther he left the Village behind him?

He entered the studio building, took the elevator to the twelfth floor, and strode down the long, familiar corridor. At the end was a large, well-lighted space in which a dozen men and women were working, set apart by partitions from the director of dramatic programs, a pock-marked redhead named Hourvitch.

Combe suddenly remembered that Hourvitch was a Hungarian, which in turn reminded him of Kay. Henceforth everything that reminded him in the slightest of Kay would have a special significance.

"I was expecting you to call yesterday," Hourvitch said, "but sit down, it doesn't matter. You're all set for Wednesday. By the way, I'm expecting your friend Laugier in a few minutes. We'll probably broadcast his new play."

The program director's phone rang. Scarcely half an hour had passed since Combe had left Kay. She had chosen his suit, tied his tie, practically dressed him. He had thought then that they were living one of life's unforgettable moments that bind two people together forever, and now it already seemed far away and unreal.

He looked around the white walls, anchoring his gaze on a big black-rimmed clock. He was trying to remember what Kay looked like, and he was having little success. He could picture her more or less the way she had looked when he first met her, her little black hat perched forward almost over her eyes, her fur thrown back from her shoulders, her cigarette ringed with lipstick, but he was annoyed—no, he

80

was worried—at not being able to envision her as she had been that morning.

His nervousness must have been visible, for the Hungarian put his hand over the mouthpiece and said, "Are you in a hurry? Aren't you going to wait for Laugier?"

Yes, he was going to wait for Laugier. But something had snapped inside him. All his calm had vanished, he could not tell at exactly what point, along with his self-confidence and a *joie de vivre* so new that he had hesitated to show it in public. And when Hourvitch at last put down the phone, Combe affected an air of nonchalance to cover up any sign of change in his mood.

"You're a Hungarian," he said, "so I suppose you know Count Larski."

"You mean the ambassador?"

"Yes, I guess he must be an ambassador by now."

"If he's the man I think you mean, he's a first-class diplomat. He's the present Hungarian Ambassador to Mexico. I knew him in Paris when he was First Secretary for a long time. I guess you know I worked in Paris for eight years with Gaumont. Larski's wife, if I remember correctly, ran away with a gigolo. . . ."

He had expected this, and he was ashamed. Those were the very words he had been looking for, that he had in fact provoked, but that now he wanted to cut short.

"That's all I wanted to know," he said.

But Hourvitch continued, "I don't know what happened to the Countess. I met her once in Cannes when I was down there on location. I was an assistant director. I thought I saw her in New York once, but I lost her in a crowd and wasn't sure." He smiled. "It wouldn't surprise me, though. You run into everybody you ever knew in New York these days, the high and the low. I suspect she'd be among the low. . . . Now about that broadcast. What I wanted to tell you was this. . . ."

Was Combe still listening? He was sorry he had come, sorry he had opened his big mouth. He was conscious of having sullied something precious, and yet it was Kay that he blamed. Why hadn't she lied about *everything* instead of mixing truth with falsehood? Had he really believed that she had been the wife of a first secretary of embassy? He didn't know any more, but he was furious. He thought bitterly, *When I get home, she'll be gone. Isn't that her routine?*

The idea of coming home to an empty apartment was so intolerable that it hurt him physically. A sharp pain stabbed his chest. He wanted to run for the elevator, to grab a taxi and hurry to the Village. Then almost instantly he thought, *I'm being silly. Of course she'll be there. Didn't she confess that the night we met, if I hadn't come along it would have been somebody else . . . ?*

A jovial voice broke into his consciousness.

"Well, well, little father, how are you?"

Combe forced a smile. He must have looked like an imbecile with that prop smile, because Laugier frowned as he shook hands.

"What's wrong, old boy? Off your feed?"

"No, not at all. Why?"

Laugier didn't frown often. Life for him was uncomplicated, or at least the complications were of his own devising. He must have been at least fifty-five, although he never admitted it. He was not married. He was constantly surrounded by pretty girls, none of them older than twenty-five, who seemed to be in constant rotation. He was like a juggler who could keep half a dozen balls in the air at once, none of which ever seemed to stay in his hands. The girls appeared and disappeared without a trace and with-

82

out leaving a ripple on the calm of his bachelor's existence. And he was always ready to share his existence with a friend. He would telephone an invitation to dinner and add, "Look, old boy, I've got a charming little girl coming to dinner too. If you're alone, I'll ask her to bring a friend. . . ."

Was Kay in the apartment? He was still worried about not being able to remember how she looked that morning. Superstitiously he thought, *It must be because she's not there.* Perhaps because of the presence of Laugier, with his good-natured cynicism, he contradicted himself immediately. *Of course, she's there. And tonight she'll have another fairy story to tell me. Why should she stop lying now?* If only he could winnow the few grains of truth from her lies. He had begun to doubt everything, even the story of the Jewish tailor and the running water at the end of the hall, which she had told him to arouse his pity. . . .

"You look peaked, old man," Laugier was saying. "Come and have a hamburger with me. Yes, I insist. It will be my pleasure. I'll be through with Hourvitch in exactly three minutes."

While the two men were settling their business, Combe found himself thinking of Kay and his wife at the same time, probably because of Hourvitch's phrase, "She ran away with a gigolo." People must have said the same thing about his wife. He didn't care. He had been sincere that morning when he declared that he no longer loved her. It was definitely not because of her that he had gone all to pieces. It was much more complicated.

Of course Kay would never understand. Why should she? It was ridiculous to put her on a pedestal just because he had been dying of loneliness the night he met her, when she was seeking, if not a man, at least a bed. Yes, it was the bed she wanted, no matter who might be in it.

"Ready, little father?"

Combe sprang up, smiling meekly.

"Hourvitch, my pretty prince," said Laugier, "you must consider our friend Combe for the part of the senator."

A small part, no doubt, but it was good of Laugier anyhow. In Paris the situation would have been reversed. Seven years ago Laugier had breezed into Fouquet's, high as a kite, to seek his help at three o'clock in the morning.

"What a part, my precious one," he had said. "Made to order for you . . . Juiciest part you ever played . . . Three hundred performances on the *boulevards* guaranteed, to say nothing of the provinces and a road company for all Europe and the Americas . . . But only if you play the duke; otherwise the whole thing flops. Without you, there's no play . . . Leave everything to me . . . I told you the gimmick . . . Now read the script and get busy . . . If you take the script to the director of the Madeleine yourself and tell him you want to play the duke, it's in the bag . . . I'll phone you tomorrow . . . Don't you agree, madame, that he ought to star in my play?"

For his wife had been with him that night. Laugier had slipped her the script with a sly smile, and next day sent her a huge box of Marquise de Sévigné chocolates. . . .

And now, seven years later . . .

"You see, old bean," Laugier was saying as the elevator took them down, "New York is like that. One day you're . . ."

Combe wanted to beg him, *Please stop. Shut up, for God's sake!* He knew the New York litany by heart, had heard it so many times. For him New York was finished. He was through thinking about it, or at least he wouldn't think about it until later. Right now there was only one thing that mattered: that there was a woman in his one-

84

room apartment, a woman he knew practically nothing about but suspected much; a woman he could observe with eyes as cold, as lucid, as cruel as had ever looked upon any woman, a woman he could despise but, he was well aware, he could not do without.

"Hourvitch is a nice guy," Laugier was saying. "He pretty well knows he stands amid the alien corn, which is only proper. He has not forgotten that he got his start sweeping out the studios at Billancourt, and he has a few little accounts to settle. Otherwise, he's a good pal, particularly when you don't need him."

Combe was on the point of stopping short, holding out his hand, and saying good-by. If ever there was a body without a soul, he was there that day on Madison Avenue. Combe walked mechanically, but he lived and thought far downtown. . . .

"You shouldn't take it so hard, old man. A month from now, maybe six weeks, you'll be the first one to laugh at the long face that's scaring the little children of Manhattan. Buck up, little old Brother, if only to show the jealous no-good bastards who aren't even worthy of yapping at your heels, that you're still on your feet. Why, I remember the night after my second play opened at the Porte-Saint-Martin . . ."

Why had she been so eager to let him go? She, whose intuition was infallible, must have known that this was not yet the moment . . . unless she herself needed the freedom. . . . He wondered whether the story of Jessie was true? Those trunks locked up in Jessie's apartment and the key on the high seas, en route to the Panama Canal. . . .

"What are you drinking?"

Laugier had guided him into a little bar rather like Kay's little bars. There was a jukebox in the corner. . . .

"A manhattan."

He thrust his hand into his pocket. While his fingers were seeking a nickel, he looked at himself in the mirror behind the glasses in back of the bar. He certainly looked ridiculous. He smiled sarcastically at his reflection.

"What are you doing after lunch?"

"I have to go home."

"Home where? I would have taken you along to a rehearsal. . . ."

Combe knew those New York rehearsals: the cast crowded into a tiny studio on the twentieth or twenty-first floor of some tower above Broadway, everything so strictly scheduled that if the rehearsal ran over the hour or two hours allotted, another troupe would come barging in while the first crew was still hard at work. He had not been impressed by the *esprit de corps*. Each member of the cast knew his own lines but little about the production as a whole. Moreover, they had little interest in their colleagues. Actors and actresses came and went without even a hello or good-by to their fellow cast members, certainly never to him. They didn't even know his name—except perhaps for a few who had been part of the same cast in previous broadcasts. When the director gave the cue, he entered, approached the mike, delivered his lines, and departed without other recognition than a titter of laughter (from the bit players) because of his French accent. He was suddenly frightened, as he sipped his manhattan. He was even panic-stricken at the thought of returning to these anonymous rehearsals, facing an impersonal mike, afraid of the titters of the snotty-nosed little bit players who didn't even know his name. No. This was a loneliness even more intense than he had suffered in his cubicle during the Friday saturnalia of Winnie and J.K.C. behind the partition.

He was scarcely aware of the fact that he had walked to the jukebox, extracted five cents from his pocket, and slipped it into the slot . . . a slot he had chosen without even thinking.

Laugier had already signaled the bartender to refill the glasses. He was listening with one ear to the singer that Combe's nickel had brought into the room. He said:

"Do you know how much money that song has earned in the United States alone? One hundred thousand dollars, my little old man! That's royalties for both the composer and lyricist, of course. But when you consider that there are thousands of jukeboxes, orchestras, night clubs, restaurants, and the radio, still playing that tune . . . well, I sometimes think I should be writing songs instead of plays." He raised his glass. "Cheerio. Shall we go in and gnaw on an old bone?"

"Would you be offended if I left you now?"

He asked the question so solemnly that Laugier not only was surprised, but for an instant forgot his usual cynicism. There was genuine concern in his voice as he said, "You really are in bad shape, aren't you?"

"Will you excuse me?"

"Of course, old man. But listen . . ."

No, he couldn't listen. He ran from the bar. Even the street noises tore at his nerves. His stupid jitters annoyed him. He stood at the bus stop for several minutes, but when a taxi came along, he flagged it down. He flung his address at the driver.

He wasn't sure which he feared the more—to find Kay at home or not to find her. He was furious with himself, furious with Kay, without knowing exactly why. He felt humiliated, terribly humiliated. The cross streets flashed past as the taxi raced downtown. He had no idea where he was, and he didn't care. He thought, *The little bitch got me out of there so she could run away without a scene.*

Then, *What did she care? Me or another? Or the gigolo at Cannes?*

When the taxi stopped, he scanned the façade of the house, as though he expected to see a change. He was pale, and he knew it. His hands were icy and his forehead beaded with cold sweat.

She was not at the window, as she had been that morning, that morning when the day was young and the sun was gay, and she had waved to him affectionately.

He ran up the stairs. He paused on the third-floor landing. He was ashamed of his anger and hoped that, by pausing for breath, he might be able to laugh at himself.

As his hand touched the banister, slightly sticky, of the last flight, where he—and she—only two hours ago . . .

He couldn't wait any longer. He banged against the door. He had to know if she was still there. He stabbed his key at the lock, missed, tried again. He was still fumbling when the door swung inward. Kay smiled at him.

"Come here," he ordered, without looking at her.

"What's the matter, darling?"

"Nothing. Come here."

She was wearing her black silk dress—the only dress she had. But she had added a little white embroidered collar he had never seen before—and it infuriated him.

"Come here."

"You know, darling, lunch is ready."

He knew that. He could see it through the open door. He could also see that the room was neat and clean for the first time in weeks. He could also imagine the bearded tailor across the street, but he preferred not to look.

Kay stared at him with even more concern than Laugier had shown. In her eyes he found the same eagerness to humor him. These fits of his apparently inspired respect. And why not? Didn't they realize that he had reached the end of his resources? If they didn't, let them say so and he would crawl off quietly to die alone in his corner. It was that simple. But he couldn't stand any more questions, any more waiting. He had had enough. . . . Enough of what? Well, questions, for one thing, especially the questions he was asking himself, that were making him physically sick, yes, sick—psychosomatic, if they insisted, but sick.

"Well?"

"I'm here, François. I just thought . . ."

She thought! She thought that she would fix him an intimate little lunch he would like. He knew that. He could see it. He wasn't blind. And after that? Was this the way he was supposed to love her, with the sanctimonious respect for the feelings of the young bride? Had they ever been able to stop before, either of them? Not he, at any rate.

"I think the hot plate . . ." she began.

The hell with the hot plate! Let it burn until they had time to think of it. Hadn't the light burned in his room for nearly forty-eight hours? Had he worried about the light?

"Come here."

What was he so afraid of? Of Kay? Of himself? Of fate? Of one thing he was certain: he was desperately in need of carrying her with him again into the anonymous crowds of Manhattan. He had to walk with her, stop here and there in little bars, rub shoulders with strangers, beg their pardon when he jostled them or stepped on their toes. Perhaps he even needed to feel his nerves grow unbearably taut while she ringed just one more "last" cigarette with her lipstick.

Did she really understand as they went down the stairs?

When they reached the sidewalk, it was he who wondered where they were going, and she who was not curious enough to ask where. So, as if resigned to whatever fate had in store for them at the moment she took his arm, he repeated dully:

"Come."

The hours that followed were exhausting. With sadistic obstinacy he insisted on going back to all the places they had been together. At the Rockefeller Center cafeteria he saw that their trays contained the same dishes exactly. He scrutinized her fiercely, and he cross-examined her bluntly and without pity.

"With whom have you been here before?"

"What do you mean?"

"Don't ask questions. Answer me. When a woman answers a question with a question, she is getting ready to lie."

"I don't understand you, François."

"You told me you came here often. You must admit that it would be unusual if you always came here alone."

"I sometimes came here with Jessie."

"That's all?"

"I don't remember."

"With a man?"

"Possibly. Yes, once, with one of Jessie's friends."

"One of Jessie's friends who just happened to be your lover?"

"Oh, now . . ."

"Admit it."

"I mean . . . well, yes, if you want to call it that. Once, in a taxi."

He could picture the inside of the cab, the impersonal shoulders of the driver, the two pale blurs of faces in the darkness. He could taste the special savor of kisses stolen almost in the very heart of a crowd.

"Bitch!"

"It was so unimportant, Frank."

Why did she have to call him Frank, all of a sudden?

"You mean it made no difference if it was he or another? One more or less?"

She shrugged. Why didn't she fight back? Her passivity, her humility, irritated him. He sprang up, seized her by the hand, dragged her from the cafeteria. Once in the street, he continued to cling to her hand as he pushed on and on, as though driven by some hidden force.

"Does this street bring back memories too? Did you walk here with a man?"

"No. I don't know any more."

"Of course. New York is such a big city, isn't it? Still, you've been living here for years. You don't expect me to believe that you haven't gone to little bars like ours, with other men, and that you haven't endlessly played other records that were at that moment *your* song. . . ."

"I've never been in love before, Frank."

"You're lying."

"Believe it or not, I've never been in love. Not the way I love you."

"You used to go to the movies. I'm sure you must have gone to the movies with a man to sit in the last row and play dirty little games in the dark. Confess!"

"I don't know any more."

"You see! It was on Broadway, wasn't it? Show me the theater."

"Maybe at the Capitol. Just once."

The Capitol was scarcely a hundred yards ahead of them. He stared at the blazing marquee.

"Who was it?"

"A young naval officer. A Frenchman."

"How long was he your lover?"

"One weekend. His ship was in Boston. He came to New York with a friend on weekend leave."

"And you took on the two of them."

"When his friend saw how things were going, he left us."

"I'll bet you picked them up on the street."

"That's right. I recognized the uniform. I overheard them speaking French. They didn't know I understood them until I smiled. Then they spoke to me."

"Which hotel did he take you to? Where did you sleep with him? Answer me!"

She remained silent.

"Answer me!"

"Why do you have to know? You're torturing yourself for nothing, I assure you. It was so unimportant, Frank."

"What hotel?"

She sighed resignedly. "The Ivy," she said.

He shouted with laughter. He dropped her arm. "That does it!" he said. "That takes the prize! Talk about the long arm of coincidence! So, on our first night—or first morning, rather, since it was nearly daylight—when I brought you to the—"

"François!"

"Yes, you're right. I'm being stupid. As you say so well, it's all so unimportant." Then, after a few steps: "I'll bet he was married, your naval officer. Did he tell you all about his wife?"

She nodded. "And he showed me pictures of his children."

He walked on, staring straight ahead, as though seeing the pictures of his own children on the wall of his bedroom. He was holding Kay's arm again. When they came opposite their little bar, he pushed her brusquely inside.

"Are you sure, absolutely sure, that you haven't come

here before with another man? You'd better admit it now."

"I've never been here with anyone but you."

"It's possible, after all, that you may be telling the truth for once."

She was not at all resentful. She was doing her best to remain her natural self. She held out her hand for a nickel and went meekly, as though performing a rite, to prod the jukebox into song.

"Two scotches."

Another round, then another and another. He pictured her in other bars with other men, begging just one last drink, lighting one last cigarette, always the last. He pictured her on the sidewalk, waiting for the man, walking awkwardly because her heels were too high and her feet hurt, taking his arm . . .

"Don't you want to go home?"

"No."

He wasn't listening to the music. He sat stolidly, apparently engaged in intensive soul-searching. Suddenly he got up and called for the check.

"Come on."

"Where are we going?"

"To look for other memories. We'll find them pretty much all over, won't we?"

As they passed a dance hall, he asked, "Do you dance?"

She misunderstood. She asked, "Do you feel like dancing?"

"I merely asked you if you dance."

"I do, François."

"Where did you go on nights when you wanted to dance? Show me. I want to know. You understand that, don't you? And if we should meet a man—are you listening to me?—a man you've slept with . . . and that is sure to happen one of these days, if it hasn't already happened. . . . I want you to do me the honor of pointing him out and saying, 'This one.'"

He gave her a sidelong glance. Her cheeks were flaming and her eyes were unnaturally bright, but he was not sorry for her. He was too unhappy himself to feel pity for her.

"Tell me. Have we already met him?"

"Of course not."

She was crying. She cried without really crying, like a little girl clinging to her mother's hand, being dragged through the crowd.

"Taxi!"

As they got in, he said, "This should give more fond memories. Who was he, this taxicab lover of yours, assuming, of course, that there was only one? It's quite the thing in New York, isn't it—love in a taxi? Who was he?"

"I already told you—a friend of Jessie's. Or rather of her husband Ronald. We met him by accident."

"Where?" He had to torture himself by visualizing everything.

"In a little French restaurant in the Forties."

"And he bought you champagne. And then Jessie discreetly withdrew, like your sailor's friend. People can be so discreet, so understanding! Let's get out here."

It was the first time since their meeting that they had come back to the corner of the all-night café.

"What do you want to do?"

"Nothing. A sentimental pilgrimage, as you see. And here?"

"What do you mean?"

"You know very well what I mean. Don't tell me that the other night was the first time you'd dropped in here for a late snack. It's just a stone's throw from where you lived with your Jessie. I'm beginning to know you well, the two of you, and I would be very much surprised if you hadn't struck up a conversation here with someone. You have quite a knack for engaging men in conversation, haven't you, Kay?"

He looked at her squarely. His face was so pale and drawn, his eyes so staring, that she didn't have the courage to protest. He tightened his grip on her arm until his fingers hurt.

"Come on."

As they passed the house where Jessie lived, Kay stopped short in surprise. There was a light burning in one of Jessie's windows.

"François, look!"

"So what? So your girl friend has come home. Unless it's your Enrico. You'd like to go up, wouldn't you? Say it. You'd like to go up?" His voice threatened. "Well, what are you waiting for? Are you afraid I might go with you and discover all the filthy little secrets that must be hidden away up there?"

This time it was she who said, in a voice heavy with unshed tears, "Come on."

She pulled him toward Fifth Avenue.

Once again they were walking up the long thorough-fare, heads down, silently, seeing nothing except the bitterness that lay between them.

"I'm going to ask you one question, Kay." He seemed calmer, more nearly in control of himself.

"I'm listening," she said, with just a hint of hope showing through her resignation.

"Promise me you'll answer me frankly."

"Of course."

"Promise?"

"I swear it."

95

"How many men have there been in your life?"

"What do you mean?"

"Don't I make myself clear?" Again his tone was aggressive, hammering.

"That depends upon what you mean when you say that a man has been in the life of a woman."

"How many men have slept with you?" He prompted her sardonically. "A hundred? A hundred fifty? More?"

"Oh no! Less, much less."

"Which means?"

"I don't know. I've never counted. Let's see . . ." She seemed to be combing her memory. Her lips moved, but he couldn't tell whether she was producing names or merely figures. "Seventeen. No, eighteen."

"Are you sure you haven't forgotten anyone?"

"I don't think so. Yes, that's all."

"Does that include your husband?"

"Sorry. No, I forgot my husband. That makes nineteen, my darling. But if you only knew how unimportant—"

"Come on."

They turned around and started back down the avenue. They were both exhausted, physically and emotionally. They said nothing; what was there to say?

Washington Square . . . The side streets of Greenwich Village . . . the light in the basement window, spotlighting a Chinese laundryman at his ironing table . . . The red-checked curtains of the Italian restaurant . . .

"Climb."

He was close behind her in the stairway, so calm, so outwardly cold that she felt goose flesh rising on the back of her neck. He opened the apartment door.

"You may go to bed," he said, as though pronouncing sentence.

"And you, darling?"

Oh yes. He. What *was* he going to do? He walked straight to the window, pressed his forehead against the pane. He heard her walking to and fro behind him. He heard the sigh of the bedsprings as she was apparently obeying instructions. He didn't move. For a long moment he remained safely protected by the armor of his bitter loneliness.

Suddenly he wheeled, strode to the bedside, and stared at her. Not a muscle in his face moved—except the ends of his lips, which whispered, "You . . ."

He repeated it, each time half a tone higher, until the word became a cry of despair.

"You . . . ! You . . . ! You . . . !"

He stared down at her face, his arm upraised. He paused, trying to regain control of himself.

"You!"

His voice broke, his arm slashed downward, his hand— or his fist; he no longer could distinguish—made a sickening sound as he struck her face. Again, again, again . . . Until he collapsed on the bed, drained at last of all energy and all substance, sobbing, begging forgiveness.

As the salt of their tears mingled on their lips, she sighed. Her voice seemed to come from far, far away as she said:

"My poor darling . . ."

chapter 6

Without knowing it they awoke very early. They were both so sure they had been sleeping for ages that neither thought of looking at the clock. It was Kay who got up first to draw the curtains, and she said:

"Look, François."

The Jewish tailor was, for the first time to their knowledge, no longer sitting cross-legged on his table. He was sitting in a chair like everybody else, a straw-bottomed chair that might have come from the hinterland of Poland or the Ukraine. He was quietly dunking thick slices of bread into some liquid in a flowered porcelain bowl. The dangling electric light, which he moved about to suit his needs, was still burning. He was eating slowly, solemnly, with no eyes for the scissors or the thick gray paper patterns hanging from his wall.

Kay said, "He's my friend. I must find some way to make him happy."

Combe nodded—because they were both happy.

"Do you know that it's only seven o'clock?" she said. No, he didn't, and neither did she. Neither of them felt any fatigue, only a profound sense of well-being that made them smile at one another for no sound reason.

She was dressing, and at the same time pouring boiling water into the coffee maker. As he watched her, he said, "There must have been somebody in your friend's apartment last night, since the light was on."

"I would be very much surprised if Jessie had come back."

"You'd like to get your clothes back, wouldn't you?" he said.

She looked at him, surprised at this generous outburst, not yet quite ready to accept it.

"Listen," he said. "I'll go back there with you, and I'll wait downstairs while you go up and investigate."

"You will?" He knew what she was thinking—that she might meet Enrico or even Ronald, Jessie's husband. "All right, let's go."

They went. The early-morning spectacle of the half-deserted streets they had not yet shared in the Village, with the provincial quiet of the thoroughfares, was not like the tired retreat of the barflies from the Times Square dawn. In the Village they seemed to be part of a fresh awakening, a cool shower for the soul, while the city was still washing its face.

"You see? There's a window open. Go on up. I'll wait here."

"I'd rather you came with me, François. Please?"

The stairway wasn't elegant, but it was clean—a solid, middle-class stairway. There were door mats in front of nearly every door, and on the second floor a maid was polishing the brass doorknob with such energy that her ample breasts quivered like gelatin. He suspected that Kay was a little frightened, and that she considered this a mutual experiment. But to him the house was commonplace and without mystery.

She rang the bell. Her lips trembled. She looked to him for assurance, furtively squeezed his hand. They could hear the bell ringing inside, but there was no answer.

"What time is it?"

"Nine o'clock."

She looked at the door of the neighboring apartment and asked, "Do you mind?" He said nothing, so she pushed the bell.

The door was opened by a man of about sixty, clad in a padded dressing gown, his scant gray hair forming a crown around his pink scalp. He held an open book in one hand, and he bowed his head to peer over the rims of his glasses.

"Well," he said. "So it's you, my little miss. I thought you'd come by, sooner or later. Was Mr. Enrico able to reach you? He stopped by last night. He asked me if you'd left your new address with me. He seemed to think you had some personal effects in the apartment that you might want to repossess."

"Thank you, Mr. Bruce. I'm sorry to have disturbed you, but I saw a light here last night, and I wanted to be sure that it was Mr. Enrico."

"No news from your little friend?"

Everything seemed so banal, so familiar.

When they were in the street again, she said, "I don't know how Enrico happens to have a key, except—yes, that must be it. In the beginning, when her husband was sent to Panama and Jessie found out she couldn't stand the climate down there and had to come back, she took an apartment in the Bronx. She got a job as a switchboard operator with a firm on Madison Avenue, and after she met Enrico—whatever you may think, they went together for five months before anything happened—he was the one who insisted she live in the Village, much closer to her job. I don't know what arrangement they had between them, but I suspect now that he was the one who paid the rent and may even have had the apartment in his name. So naturally he would have a key. . . ."

"Why don't you phone him?"

"Phone who?"

"Enrico, my girl. Since he has a key, and all your belongings are locked up in this apartment, what could be more natural?"

"You really want me to phone him?"

He squeezed her hand. "Please do."

He locked his arm in hers and marched her to the nearest drugstore—where she suddenly remembered that Jessie's lover never got to work before ten o'clock. So they sat at the counter, as unconcerned as an old married couple, waiting.

Twice she shut herself in the phone booth, and twice returned unsuccessful. On the third attempt she apparently made contact with her past. He could watch her through the glass door as she talked, and, although her past was at the other end of the wire, her eyes never left François Combe. She smiled at him continuously, timidly, as though she were thanking him and asking his forgiveness all at once.

"He's coming down," she announced. "I hope you don't mind. I couldn't put him off. He said he'd jump in a taxi and be here in ten minutes. He couldn't say very much because there was somebody in his office, but he said a messenger brought him the key in an envelope that had Ronald's name on it."

So they waited on the sidewalk. He wondered if she would take his arm in the presence of the South American. She did—just as the taxi drew up. She looked at Combe squarely so that he could see the promise shining in her eyes. She wanted him to see that her eyes were clear and candid, and that the pleading pout of her lips asked his indulgence and his courage.

He needed neither. He felt suddenly so objective that he had a hard time keeping a straight face.

This Enrico, or Ric, as he liked to be called, was a little, unprepossessing fellow of whom nobody could be jealous. He was not ugly, exactly, but he was so commonplace, so obviously small potatoes, that he himself felt obliged to run up to Kay dramatically, to seize both her hands and exclaim effusively:

"My poor Kay! That all this should happen to us!"

Very simply she introduced the men. "Enrico, I want you to meet a friend of mine, François Combe. You may speak freely, because I've told him everything."

Combe noted that she addressed Enrico with the intimate second-person singular.

"Let's go right up," said Enrico. "I have an important appointment in my office in fifteen minutes. I'm keeping the cab."

Enrico went up the stairs first, leaving a faint trace of perfume in his wake. He was quite a small man, perfectly groomed. And Combe thought he detected the marks of a curling iron in his well-pomaded hair.

Enrico looked for the key on an impressive-looking key ring—to Combe's delight; he hated men who carried key rings—and finally found what he was seeking in a vest pocket. During the search his feet, in shoes as flexible as dancing pumps, beat a nervous tattoo on the floor. He spoke in a French of sorts:

103

"What a catastrophe when I came here and found nobody! Luckily I thought of ringing the bell of the nice old gentleman next door. He gave me the note she'd left for me."

"For me too," Kay said.

"I know. He told me. I didn't know where to find you." He stole a glance at Combe, who smiled at him. Perhaps he was expecting an explanation from Kay. All he got was a happy smile.

"Then yesterday I got the key. Just the key, no explanation. So I came down last night."

Lord, how simple it all was! And how prosaic! The open window was causing a draft, and Enrico closed the door as soon as they were all inside. It was a small, ordinary apartment, no different from thousands of others in New York, with the same overstuffed sofa, the same coffee table, the same ash trays beside each armchair, the same record player, the same miniature library in a corner cabinet next to the window. It was here that Kay and Jessie . . .

Combe smiled unconsciously, a smile that seemed to come from deep inside. There may have been a trace of malice in his eyes, but just a trace, and he wondered if Kay was annoyed by it. What picture had he been building for himself of the life she had been leading here, of these men she was eternally calling by their first names, which made him wince? Well, one of the men stood before him now, and he could not help noticing that at ten o'clock in the morning he was wearing a pearl stickpin in his gaily colored tie.

After closing the window Kay went into the bedroom. "Would you give me a hand, François darling?"

The "darling" was for Enrico's benefit; she wanted him to know how things stood between her and Combe.

104

She had glanced into an old trunk, then swung open a closet door.

"But Jessie didn't take any of her things with her!" was her surprised exclamation.

"Yes, I know," Enrico said. "This morning I got a letter she wrote on the *Santa Clara*."

"Then she's already at sea?"

"He made her take the first boat to Panama with him. It wasn't as bad as I thought it might have been. When he arrived, he knew exactly what was going on. I'll let you read the letter. He didn't let her out of his sight. How she managed to write at all I'll never know. Anyhow, when he walked into the apartment, he said, 'Are you alone?' She said, 'You can see for yourself.' 'Aren't you expecting him any moment now?'"

Enrico was holding his cigarette in the self-conscious manner of so many American girls. He said, "You know Jessie. She didn't say so in her letter, but she must have protested, grown indignant, thrown her arms around. . . ."

Combe looked at Kay. They both smiled.

"It seems Ronald was very cold."

Well, well! So Enrico called him Ronald too.

"I wonder if he didn't come to New York just to try to catch her in the act. I don't know who might have tipped him off. Anyhow, while Jessie was swearing to God that he was completely off his nut, he walked straight to the closet, grabbed my pajamas and dressing gown, and threw them on the bed."

They were still there. The dressing gown was a thing of wonder, with huge floral patterns, and the pajamas were of cream-colored silk with initials embroidered in dark red.

"While she was crying," Enrico continued, "Ronald went through all her things. He picked out all the dresses that were hers three years before, when she came back from

105

Panama. Those she could take with her. The rest she had to leave behind. You know Jessie. . . ."

Combe himself was beginning to know Jessie. Furthermore, Kay herself was beginning to be more understandable, so much so that he felt a little sheepish.

"You know Jessie. She couldn't bear the idea of parting with some of the dresses and things she had acquired in the past three years. She said, 'But I swear, Ronald, that I bought these things with my own money.'"

Could it be that Enrico actually had a sense of humor?

"I don't know how she managed to write me all this with her husband spying on her every minute of the day, as she said, but she did write six pages—in pencil. There was a message for you, too, Kay. She said that she was giving you everything that she couldn't pack, and that you were welcome to wear anything you needed."

"Thank you, Enrico, but I couldn't do that."

"The rent on the apartment is paid until the end of the month. I don't know yet what I'll do with all my stuff here. I can't take it home, as you know. If you want, I'll leave you the key. I'll have to leave it with you anyhow, since I have to go now. I really have some very important meetings this morning. I suppose that now they're on the high seas, Ronald will leave her in peace."

"Poor Jessie!"

Did Enrico feel any guilt at all? He said, "I wonder if there is anything *I* might have done. I had no idea that there was a crisis in the making. That night my wife was giving a big dinner, so I couldn't even telephone Jessie. . . . Good-by, Kay. Send the key to my office when you're through with it."

Enrico didn't know exactly how he should treat this man he scarcely knew, but he shook his hand with exaggerated warmth, and then, as though his seal of approval was necessary, said, "Take good care of this girl. She's Jessie's best friend."

"What's the matter with you, François?"

"Nothing, my darling."

It was the first time he had called her darling without a trace of sarcasm. Perhaps having found Enrico to be such a little man had reduced Kay's stature, too, but not unfavorably. In fact, he felt for her only an infinite tenderness.

The little man had gone, leaving behind only a faint, lingering scent, his pajamas and dressing gown on a bed, and his slippers on the floor of the open closet.

"Now do you understand?" Kay asked.

"I do indeed." It was true. He was glad he had come. He finally saw her in her proper perspective, in her own setting, and all these men—the Enricos, the Ronalds, the sailors, these friends with whom indifferently she used the intimate second-person singular—he saw them in their correct dimensions.

He did not love her any less for it. On the contrary, he loved her with deeper affection, with less strain and bitterness. He had almost lost his fear of her and of the future. Perhaps he had lost all fear and could let himself go at last.

"Sit down," she said. "You take up too much room."

Had this bedroom she had shared with Jessie become smaller too, like everything else in his eyes? It was a gay, pleasant little room. The walls were off-white, the cretonne spreads on the twin beds were imitation Jouy print. So were the drapes, through which the sun was filtering. He sat down obediently on the bed next to the flowered dressing gown.

"I was right, wasn't I, to refuse to take any of Jessie's things? Look, do you like this dress?"

107

It was an evening gown that seemed to him quite pretty, and she held it up in front of her like a Fifth Avenue salesgirl tempting a customer.

"Have you worn it often?" It was not a jealous question this time. He merely wanted to show his interest and his appreciation of her naïve display of innocent coquetry.

"Only twice. And neither time, I swear, did anybody touch me. Nobody even kissed me."

"I believe you."

"Truly?"

"I believe you."

"There are the shoes to wear with it. The gold is a little gaudy for my taste. I wanted some in old gold, but these were all I could find in my price range. Am I boring you with my fashion show?"

"No indeed."

"Sure?"

"On the contrary. Come and kiss me."

She hesitated, out of some sort of respect for his new mood. Then she bent over and quickly brushed his lips with hers.

"Do you know that you're sitting on my bed?"

"What about Enrico?"

"He only slept here about twice a month, sometimes less. He had to invent a business trip as an excuse for his wife. And it was complicated even then, because she always wanted to know the name of the hotel so she could phone him. She wouldn't have hesitated to call in the middle of the night."

"Did she suspect something?"

"I think she did, but she pretended not to know. She took care of herself in her own way. I don't think she ever loved him, or at any rate, she had stopped loving him, but that didn't stop her from being jealous. If she had tried to do anything rash, though, he was quite capable of divorcing her to marry Jessie."

So the little fellow with the pearl stickpin would tolerate no nonsense? It was good to be able to listen calmly to all this now, and to be able automatically to give words and things their proper weight.

"He used to come over often to spend the evening. Every two or three days. He had to leave for home around eleven o'clock on those nights, and often I would go to the movies to leave them alone. I'll show you the theater. It's right near here. Sometimes I would sit through the same film three times rather than take the subway uptown."

"Aren't you dying to put on that dress?"

"How did you know?" She still held it in her hands. With a deft movement he had never seen before she slipped out of the black dress she had been wearing for days. He had the curious impression of seeing her for the first time in her underthings. In fact, had he ever really looked at her undressed?

Even better, he had not even been curious about her body. His body had known hers in the most intimate and violent contact. Only last night they had again wallowed in the abyss. His tactile knowledge of her could not be more complete. And yet he did not know how she was built; visually he could not have described her body.

"Should I change everything, darling?"

"Everything, *chérie*."

"Go lock the door."

It was almost like a game, a most enjoyable game. This was the third bedroom they had entered together and in each he had found not only a different Kay but different reasons for loving her and a different way of loving her.

He sat down again on the edge of the bed and watched her undress. She was naked now, and her skin was

109

very white except where the morning sun touched it with pale gold. She was digging into a drawerful of lingerie.

"I wonder what I should do about my things at the laundry," she said. "They'll bring it here and there'll be nobody home. Maybe we'd better stop by the laundry. Do you mind?"

He liked the way she said, "*We'd* better stop by," not just "I," as though they were always to be together from now on.

"Jessie had much prettier lingerie than I have. Look at this." She rubbed the flimsy silk with her fingers, held it out for him to feel. "Jessie had a much better figure than mine, too. Do you want me to put on this slip? Or is it too pink for your taste? Oh, I've got a black slip and step-ins too. I always wanted black undies and I finally bought some. I've never had the courage to wear them, though. I've always been afraid it would make me feel like a tart."

She was combing her hair. She knew exactly, without looking, where to reach for the comb. Her hand found the mirror automatically. She had a pin between her teeth as she said, "Would you hook me up behind?"

She'd never asked him to do that before. What an amazing number of things they were doing for the first time this morning! For instance, it was the first time he had kissed the back of her neck, gently, without greediness, merely for the pleasure of breathing the fragrance of her hair, where it curled close to the nape. Then he went back to sit on the edge of the bed like a good boy.

"Do you like the dress?"

"It's very becoming."

"I bought it on Fifty-seventh Street. It was very expensive, you know—at least for me." She gave him a beseeching look. "Maybe we could go out together some night. You could dress up and I could wear this dress.

. . ." Then, without transition, while her lips were still smiling, two big tears rolled from under her eyelids. She turned her head away as she said, "You've never asked me what I did for a living."

It was a curious question from a woman in an evening gown, standing with bare feet in golden slippers.

"And I never dared talk about it myself," she went on, "because the subject was humiliating. I guess I was stupid, but I preferred to let you imagine things. In fact, I even did it on purpose at times."

"Did what on purpose?"

"You know very well what! When I first met Jessie, I was working in the same building. That's how we met— we used to eat lunch at the same drugstore downstairs. I'll show it to you someday; it's on the corner of Madison Avenue. I was hired as a translator, because I knew several languages.

"Only there's something you don't know. It's ridiculous and I'm ashamed of it. I told you a little about my life with my mother. When she began to be famous as a virtuoso and spent most of her time on the road, I practically stopped going to school. Oh, I spent a few months in this school or that, between seasons, but I didn't learn very much. Especially—now, don't you dare laugh!—I never learned to spell. Larski used to tell me—and I'm humiliated all over again every time I think of that cold voice of his —that I wrote like a scullery maid.

"So now you know. Unhook me in back, will you, please?"

She offered him her back, pale, lean, and appetizing between the dark shoulder straps. When his fingers stroked her skin, she begged:

"No, please, not right now. Do you mind? I'd like so much to talk some more."

She stepped out of the evening gown. Clad only in panties and bra, she sought her cigarette case and her lighter, sat cross-legged on Jessie's bed, and pulled an ash tray within reach.

"They transferred me to the mailing department," she went on. "Two other girls and I worked all day long in a stuffy cell with no window, back of the offices, stuffing circulars into envelopes, sticking on addresses. The two girls were little animals. We had nothing in common. They hated me. We wore smocks because of the oceans of glue. I insisted on a clean smock every day. . . . But I'm boring you. This is all ridiculous, isn't it?"

"Not at all."

"You just say that. Well, you asked for it. Every morning, I'd find my clean smock already smeared with glue, even on the inside, where I'd get it on my dress. I had a real fight with one of them, a big Irish girl with a face like a Kalmuck. She weighed more than I did. She ruined a brand-new pair of stockings."

"My poor Kay!" he said. His voice was at once pitying and gay.

"Maybe you think I was trying to be the wife of a first secretary of embassy. That's not true. I swear it. If Jessie were here, she could tell you."

"But I believe you, darling."

"I admit that I couldn't face it. I ran away from those two brats. I thought finding another job would be easy, but it wasn't. I was out of work for three weeks. That's when Jessie suggested that I move in with her. She was living in the Bronx then; I think I told you: a big barracks of an apartment house with iron fire escapes crawling up and down the brick walls. The building always smelled of cabbage cooking from top to bottom. For months we went to sleep and woke up with the taste of cabbage in our mouths. . . . Still, I had no rent money and Jessie had the bed. . . .

"I finally got a job in a Broadway movie house. Remember yesterday, when you were asking me about the movies. . . ." There were again tears in her eyes. "I was an usherette—not much of a job, you'll say. I know I'm not particularly strong, since I spent two years in a TB sanatorium. But the other girls had no more stamina than I. At night we were all ready to drop. Or sometimes it was just the vertigo produced by the maddening music, the magnified voices coming out of the walls, the endless walking up and down the aisles. Dozens of times I've seen the girls faint—but never on the floor. If they had the bad manners to pass out in public, they were out of a job. Bad public relations, you understand. . . . Am I boring you?"

"No. Come here."

She came closer to sit opposite him on the other twin bed. He caressed her, and was surprised to find her flesh so soft. Between the top of her step-ins and the line of her bra, there were contours that were new to him, shadows that stirred him strangely.

"I was very ill. Four months ago I had to go to the hospital for seven weeks. Only Jessie came to see me. They wanted to send me away to another sanatorium, but I refused. Jessie begged me to stay home and rest for a while before trying to get work again. When I met you, I'd been job-hunting for about a week." She smiled defiantly. "I'll find one, too." Then, without transition, "Wouldn't you like a drink? There must be a bottle of whisky in the cupboard—unless Ronald drank it, which would surprise me very much."

She went into the next room, returned with a bottle three-fourths empty. She put it down and disappeared into

113

the kitchen. He heard her open the refrigerator and exclaim, "Well, if that doesn't beat all."

"What's wrong?"

"You'll laugh. Ronald remembered to turn off the refrigerator. It couldn't have been Enrico yesterday; he wouldn't have thought of it. It's just like Ronald. You heard what Jessie wrote. Always cool and collected. No scenes. He was the one who sorted her things and told her what she could take along. And you'll notice that he left nothing lying around, either. Everything put back in place —except Enrico's robe and pajamas. Don't you think that's funny?"

No, he didn't think it was funny. He didn't think anything. He was happy. It was a new kind of happiness. If anyone had told him yesterday, or even this morning, that he would find pleasure in lolling about lazily, voluptuously, in this bedroom he had never seen before, he would not have believed it. He lay stretched on the bed that had been Kay's, squinting into a ray of sunshine, his hands clasped behind his head, gently drinking in the surroundings, detail by detail, like a painter laboring over the minutiae of a too specific canvas.

He was doing the same with Kay, unhurriedly, bit by bit, filling in her complete personality.

A little later, when he got energy enough to move, he would get up and take a look at the kitchen, even peek into the refrigerator, curious about what little clues he might find.

There were photographs on the bureau, Jessie's no doubt, among them a buxom, dignified old lady who was probably her mother. He would ask Kay about it. She could talk her head off now about the past and he would not be bored.

"Drink."

114

She tipped up the glass for him, then withdrew it to drink from it herself.

"You see, François, it's not so glamorous after all. You were so wrong. . . ."

Wrong about what? It was such a vague expression, and yet he understood it.

"Move over a little, will you?"

She slid down beside him. She was almost naked and he was fully clothed, but it seemed to make no difference. As he took her into his arms, their contact could not have been more intimate had they both been nude. Her lips were close to his ear as she whispered, "You know, darling, nothing has ever happened to me here before. I swear it."

He was without physical desire, without passion. He would have to go back a long way, even to his boyhood perhaps, to recapture a sensation that was of such unalloyed sweetness as the one that overwhelmed him now. He caressed her. It was not her flesh that he was caressing; it was all of her, a Kay whose whole being was becoming part of his, just as his was being absorbed in hers. They lay for a long time like this, not speaking, body and soul intermingled, their eyes half closed yet so near each other's that the glow of ineffable ecstasy was almost tangible.

For the first time he was not worried about possible consequences. He saw her pupils widen, her lips part slightly. He felt her breath on his cheek. He heard her voice, as from afar, saying, "Thank you, darling."

There was no fear this time that rancor or bitter afterthoughts might follow passion spent. When their bodies disentwined, they could look one another squarely in the eye without shame or regret. A wonderful weariness made their every gesture like something from a slow-motion film.

115

The shaft of sunlight that lay across the bed was like a scarf of gold created especially for them. . . .

"Where are you going, François?"

"To look in the refrigerator."

"Are you hungry?"

"No."

For half an hour or more he had been planning to inspect the kitchen. It was neat and clean, freshly painted. He opened the refrigerator. Inside were a slice of cold meat, some grapefruit, several overripe tomatoes, and a cube of butter wrapped in wax paper.

He picked up the meat with his fingers, dangled it above his mouth, and bit into it, grinning like a kid eating an apple stolen from a neighbor's orchard.

He was still grinning and still chewing when he followed Kay into the bathroom.

"You see? You *were* hungry," Kay said.

Still grinning, he shook his head stubbornly. "No."

Then he laughed heartily at her puzzled expression.

chapter 7

Two days later he went to the studio for his broadcast. He was playing a Frenchman again, a faintly ridiculous part. Hourvitch did not even shake hands with him. The Hungarian was very much the busy director, every inch the big boss, rushing about the studio with his shirt sleeves rolled up, his red hair standing on end, his secretary rushing after him, notebook in hand.

"What do you expect me to do, old man?" he shouted at Combe. "Get yourself a telephone, at least, and leave your number with my casting people so they can get in touch with you when a better part comes along. It's inconceivable that there are still people in New York without a phone."

Combe was unruffled. Nothing could disturb his serenity. He had left Kay for the first time in . . . How many days had it been, incidentally? Seven? Eight? Numbers

117

meant nothing. They were ridiculous. Any way you figured, they would add up to eternity.

He had wanted to bring her with him to the studio. She could sit in the waiting room until after the broadcast. She had refused.

"No, *mon chéri*. It's all right for you to leave me *now*."

They had both laughed over the *now*, which meant so much to them.

"I'll be home at six," he had promised.

"It doesn't matter, François. Come home whenever you like."

Why, then, since she had asked for no promise, had he persisted in repeating, "Six o'clock at the latest?"

And here he was already breaking his promise. At least, he felt very guilty when, instead of waiting for his bus, he found himself walking into the gathering dusk in the direction of the Ritz Bar.

He knew what he was looking for at the Ritz and he was not very proud of it. Every evening around six Laugier held court at the Ritz Bar, surrounded by members of New York's French colony, Frenchmen passing through, or figures from the international artistic set on their way to or from Paris, London, Rome, Berlin, or Hollywood. The bar had something of the same atmosphere as Fouquet's. When he had first come to the United States, when he was not sure that he was going to stay or even that he would be able to make his living there, reporters had run him down at the Ritz Bar and had taken his picture.

He knew what he would find there, but he was not sure why he had come. Was it some inner need of betraying Kay, of giving full vent to the evil things that still fermented within him, of getting even with Kay? Getting even for what? During the days and the nights they had spent together, he had worked desperately to wall themselves off from the world, to create the absolute privacy he thought necessary to create complete intimacy between them, to annihilate the most elementary factors of shyness and modesty that exist even between persons of the same sex, even in the promiscuities of the barracks. He had gone with her to do the shopping in the morning, he had helped her set the table, he had drawn the water for her bath, he had— He had done everything, fiercely determined to establish this absolute intimacy. Why, then, at the hour of six, when she was expecting him, when he had insisted that she should expect him, was he breezing into the Ritz Bar, instead of jumping on a downtown bus or getting a taxi?

"Hello, little father. Greetings. Draw up a chair."

It was certainly not this easy familiarity that he was seeking. He had always detested this sort of thing. Was it to reassure himself that the leash was not too tight, that he still retained some freedom of movement, that after all, he remained François Combe?

Half a dozen people were sitting at the two round tables that Laugier had pulled together. His offhand friendliness always made it difficult to distinguish his old cronies from people he had just met for the first time. It was just as difficult to keep track of who was buying the next round and whose hat was whose among those piled atop the coatrack.

"May I present . . ."

It was an American girl, quite pretty, a cover girl possibly, who had just imprinted her lipstick on a fresh cigarette.

Laugier was making the rounds, repeating at intervals, "One of our must personable, charming, and celebrated actors of the Paris stage, whose name I'm sure you know, François Combe."

One of those introduced was a rat-faced Frenchman
—Combe didn't know why he disliked him instinctively,
but he was sure that the man must be a crooked financier
or a dubious industrialist—who couldn't keep his eyes off
the actor.

"I had the pleasure of meeting your wife a few weeks
ago, during a gala at the Lido. Wait. I just happen to have
in my pocket . . ."

He produced a French newpaper that had just reached
New York. Combe had not looked at a French newspaper
for months. On Page 1 there was a picture of his wife:
"Marie Clairois, charming and talented star of . . ."

Combe was not upset, no matter what Laugier
thought. Laugier was giving him a series of eye and eye-
brow signals, all calling for calm. He *was* calm. To prove
it, after the courtiers had drunk their quota of cocktails and
departed, and Combe was left alone with his friend, it was
of Kay that he spoke:

"I want you to do me a favor. I want you to find a job
for a girl I know."

"How old is she, this girl?"

"I don't know exactly. Say, thirty, maybe thirty-
three."

"In New York, old man, that's no longer considered
a girl."

"Meaning what?"

"That the odds are against her. Forgive me for putting
it so crudely, because I suspect a special interest. Good-
looking?"

"That depends on your point of view."

"The old story. She started out as a chorus girl four-
teen or fifteen years ago, no? She grabbed the gold ring and
she dropped it. Yes?"

Combe retreated into silence. Laugier may have been

sorry for him at that instant, but Laugier's view of the world was exclusively a Laugier's-eye view.

"What can she do, your lovely virgin?"

"Nothing."

"Now don't get steamed up, dear boy. I'm looking at this for your own good, as well as hers. In New York, there's no time to play hide-and-seek. Seriously, I'm asking you: what's her line?"

"And seriously, I'm telling you: nothing."

"Can't she develop into a secretary? A phone operator? A model? A . . . I don't know what. Anything?"

Combe was going about this in the wrong way. It was his fault. He was already paying the price of his little betrayal.

"Listen to me, little father . . . Waiter, the same."

"Not for me."

"Shut up! I've got to talk to you, man to man, eye to eye, friend to friend. Understand? When you walked in here a little while ago with that undertaker's face of yours, I tuned you in right away. And the last time we met, when we left Hourvitch, don't you think I got your wave length right off? So? Your girl has a New York age of thirty, thirty-three. That means thirty-five in good French. . . . Do you want me to give you some good advice, which you will turn your back on so fast that you'll bust a gut? Well, here's the advice, right on the line: Get rid of her, little old brother!"

Combe was silent.

"And since I'm talking into the wind," Laugier went on, "may I ask just where you two stand?"

Combe was stupidly furious, furious with himself, furious at feeling like a little boy as he stood in front of Laugier, who obviously felt seven feet tall.

"Nowhere," he said.

"Then why are you getting yourself into such a stew? There's no brother, is there? No husband, no lover to blackmail you? There's no charge of kidnaping, is there?

Why didn't he have the courage to get up and get out? Did those few drinks make a coward of him? If their love were to be at the mercy of four or five cocktails . . .

"Don't you want to talk seriously?" Combe asked.

"But I am talking seriously, my little old man. Or rather, I've been joking, but when I joke, that's when I'm the most serious. This little mouse of yours, this thirty-three-year-old mouse with no job, no profession, no talent, and no bank account—let's face it, she's through. I don't have to take you over to the Waldorf to prove my point. This is the men's bar, but just step through the door, cross the corridor, and you'll see fifty girls, one prettier than the other, all of them between eighteen and twenty, some of them even virgins, and every last one of them in the same shape as your old virago of thirty-three. In a little while, forty-eight of the fifty will walk out of here wearing a thousand dollars' worth of jewelry and smart clothes, they'll go to some Automat and dine on a fifteen-cent sandwich with maybe a nickel's worth of what they call here 'French fries' doused with free ketchup. Then they'll go home to bed, God knows where. Look, did you come to this country to work, or what?"

"I don't know."

"Well, if you don't know, get the hell back to France and sign the first contract they offer you at the Renaissance or the Port-Saint-Martin. I know that you're going to do exactly what you want, that you'll never forgive me for trying to give you advice, that you already hate my guts. But you're not the first friend I've seen land here and take a nose dive.

"Now listen. If you make up your mind to hang onto

the wheel and never mind the bumps, I'm with you. But if you insist on doing an amateur-night Romeo and Juliet, then I must bid you good-by, old boy. Waiter!"

"No, wait. This is my—"

"Nonsense. I've been yelling at you enough to give me the right to buy you a few drinks. What story does she tell, your little mouse? She's a divorcee, of course. At that age, they've all been divorced at least once."

Why, exactly, had Kay been divorced?

"She's been around, hasn't she? A rolling stone who's decided it's time to gather a little moss."

"You're wrong, really."

He didn't have the strength to go on betraying Kay.

"Can you swim?"

"A little."

"Good. A little. Enough to reach shore if the sea is calm and the water not too cold. But if you had to save yourself *and* a panic-stricken madwoman who grabbed you, hung on for dear life, and fought furiously because she was afraid you would let her go down? Well, answer me?"

Combe said nothing. Laugier signaled the waiter for another round.

"Well, old boy, she's going to fight and flounder furiously, believe me! And you'll sink together like two stones. Day before yesterday when you left me, I didn't want to mention this, because you had a chip on your shoulder and you wanted to kick somebody's teeth in—anybody's. Today you seem more rational."

Combe bit his lip.

"When I saw you march up to that jukebox like you were approaching an altar, stick your coin in the slot, and wait for the record to drop, with a look in your eyes like a *midinette* about to swoon at the sight of a matinee idol . . . No, old man, no! Not you! Not you or me; we live with that business and we know what makes it tick. So let me repeat for the last time, and I'm talking like an old chum who'd give the world to help you—François, you're sunk!"

Laugier counted his change, emptied his glass, calculated the tip, and stood up. "Which way are you going?"

"I'm going home."

"Home! Where there's not even a telephone. And you expect the producers to run after you?"

They went out in single file and stood on the Madison Avenue sidewalk, where the doorman held a taxi for them.

"You see, little brother, at home in Paris the lucky number comes up just once. Here you might get a chance to play it twice, three times. But don't stretch your luck too far. I can show you cuties who started out in the chorus line or behind a typewriter at sixteen, had a Rolls-Royce and a chauffeur at eighteen, and were back in the chorus at twenty-two—starting all over again at zero. I've known some who have hit the jackpot two, three times, and who went back to the footlights after losing a Park Avenue penthouse and a yacht in Florida—and who managed to get themselves still another husband.

"This gal of yours—has she managed to keep her jewelry, at least?"

Combe didn't deign to reply. What could he have said?

"If you listen to me, you'll try to get her a job as usherette in a movie house. And even that! Maybe with proper sponsors . . . You could kill me, couldn't you? Too bad. But much better for you. Everybody hates the surgeon who's just carved him up. You're too good for all this silly business, old ham bone, and when you realize it, you'll be cured. By-by."

Combe had had too much to drink. He had not realized it before because of the rapid rhythm of round after round, of the noise in the bar, and the suspense of his long wait for the chance to talk to Laugier alone.

He remembered his wife's photo on the front page of the Paris newspaper, the light making a blur of her hair, her head a little too large for her shoulders. The film people had always said that these were features that allowed her to play young roles—that and the fact that she had never had any hips. . . .

Was Laugier blessed with second sight, or did he know about Kay. *Usherette in a movie house. And even that* . . . ! Even that indeed! Poor Kay, with her strength still sapped by her long fight back to health!

Here you might get a chance to play it twice, three times . . .

The thought struck him as he walked through the patches of light that slanted down from the Madison Avenue shop windows. Kay had been gambling. He was her last chance. He was the lucky number that had come up at the very last minute. Had he come in fifteen minutes later, or perhaps sat down on another stool at the owl café, perhaps one of the drunken sailors would have . . .

Suddenly she was very dear to him. As a reaction against his cowardice, he hurried his homeward steps. He wanted to reassure her, to tell her that not all the Laugiers in the world, with their easy sophistication and their haughty cynicism, could prevail against the deep affection he shared with her.

He must be drunker than he thought, he reflected as he bumped a passer-by and raised his hat ridiculously high in apology. But he was sincere, anyhow. The rest of them, all the Laugiers—like the rat-faced Frenchman who after the second drink had made a triumphant exit with the Ameri-

125

can girl—the whole gang from the Ritz Bar, like the gang at Fouquet's—they were a bunch of assholes . . . !

He liked the phrase, which he had dug up from the depths of his memory. He liked it so well he repeated it aloud as he walked along:

"They're a bunch of assholes." The sound made him even more furious. "Assholes, that's all they are. I'll show them!"

What would he show them? He didn't know, but it mattered so little. He'd show them. He didn't need Laugier or Hourvitch—Hourvitch, who hadn't shaken hands and had barely seemed to recognize him—he didn't need any of them any more. Nobody . . . !

Assholes!

His wife, too. She had no need to play her number twice, three times. Her number had come up the first time, but it wasn't enough for her. She had to use her luck, to use him, to make a career for a gigolo! It was the truth. When he had promoted her to play opposite him, she was nothing. She didn't exist. She played walk-ons, or maybe a bit part, like the maid who clumsily opens the sliding doors to the dining room and stammers in a frightened voice, "Dinner is served, *Madame la Comtesse*."

And he had made her over into Marie Clairois. Even the name was his creation; he had made it up. Her real name was Thérèse Bourcicault, and her father sold shoes in the market place of a little town in the Jura Mountains. He remembered the night he had rechristened her. They were eating lobster *à l'américaine* in a little restaurant with red-checkered tablecloths on the Avenue de Clichy . . . La Crémaillère, that was it.

"Marie is such a French name," he had said. "Not only French, but universal. In fact, it's become such a common name that nobody but a nursemaid would use the name

Marie these days. So now it has become original again. Marie."

She had asked him to repeat the name.

"Marie . . . And now, Clairois . . ." He remembered that creating a rationale for Clairois had been more complicated. To make Clairois out of *clairon* was a little farfetched. . . .

Tonnerre de Dieu! What the devil was he thinking of? He didn't give a damn about La Clairois and her gigolo who was going to make a name for himself only because he had cuckolded the great Combe!

And the other one, the self-satisfied, condescending idiot who spoke of the jewelry Kay didn't have and of a nice little job as usherette . . .

If she had good sponsors!

It was only a few weeks ago that Laugier had asked him, with the monumental conceit of a man half convinced that he is God the Father:

"How long can you hold out, dear boy?"

"That depends on what you mean."

"Enough to have your suits pressed every day, to pay your laundry, rent, and meals, with enough pocket money for taxis and a few cocktails."

"Five months, maybe six. When my son was born, I took out an endowment policy that would pay for his college education when he reached eighteen. I suppose I could borrow on it, or maybe turn it in. . . ."

Laugier wasn't interested in Combe's son.

"Five or six months, good! Get yourself a place to live, any place, even a dump, as long as it's got a telephone. . . ."

And today Hourvitch had told him the same thing! But he wasn't going to be bothered by this coincidence. Not today. He should have taken the bus. The traffic wasn't

127

so bad at this hour. And a few minutes more or less wouldn't make any difference if Kay were going to worry. . . .

Kay!

What a different sound the name had then, and two hours ago, three hours, that morning, at noon when they were sitting face to face over lunch, smiling at the little tailor across the street to whom Kay had had delivered, anonymously, a beautifully roasted capon. They had been so happy! The name Kay made a happy sound. Even now it was soothing. . . .

He decided to take a taxi. The sky had grown so black, so menacing as it shrouded the tops of the skyscrapers, even though it reflected the glow of the city. He leaned back gloomily against the cushions as he gave his address to the driver. He resented Laugier. He resented Rat-face. He resented everybody. He was not even sure but that he might resent Kay. He was still scowling as the cab drew up to his curb, and he got out.

He had not had time to recapture a gayer mood and a lover's expression before he saw Kay. She was waiting for him on the sidewalk, out of breath, her face haggard.

"At last, François! Come quickly! Michèle . . ." Then without transition she began frantically to speak German.

He had been up and down the stairs three times, and it was nearly midnight. Each time the street lights had seemed dimmer, the stairway dingier, his room more oppressive. His topcoat was soaked, his face cold and dripping with rain. The storm had broken suddenly.

The question of the telephone was still pursuing him. This time it was Kay who had said, testily, in fact, but he could hardly blame her, with the state she was in, "Why don't you have a phone?"

It was because there was no phone in the apartment that Enrico had come himself to bring the telegram. Another coincidence: he had come at almost the very minute that Combe was entering the Ritz Bar and feeling a little guilty. If he had come right home, as he had promised . . .

This time he was not jealous of Enrico, even though Kay may have cried on his shoulder and he had probably tried to comfort her.

Another coincidence: the day before while they were shopping for dinner Kay had said, "Maybe I ought to give my new address to the post office. It's not that I get much mail, you know, but . . ." She tried not to make him jealous. "I ought to give Enrico the address, too, just in case . . ."

"Why don't you telephone him?" Combe had asked.

He could not then foresee the importance of his remark. They stepped into the drugstore, as they had done previously. He watched her through the glass panel. He could see her lips move but could not hear what she was saying.

He had not been jealous.

Just that day Enrico had gone to Jessie's place for his things. He found some mail for Jessie and the telegram for Kay. Since the telegram came from Mexico and was already a day old, he brought it to her. She was fixing dinner, and wore a pale-blue negligee that made her look like a bride.

MICHELE SERIOUSLY ILL MEXICO CITY STOP
BANK OF COMMERCE AND INDUSTRY AUTHORIZED
ADVANCE YOU TRAVEL EXPENSES IF NECESSARY
LARSKI

He was not telling her to come. He had left her free to make her own decision. Suspecting that she might be short of money, however, he had coldly and methodically made the proper arrangements.

"I didn't even know that he had sent for Michèle. I hadn't heard in four months."

"Heard from whom?"

"From my daughter. She doesn't write often. I suspect that she's been forbidden to write to me and has to do it secretly, although she has never said so. Her last letter came from Hungary and said nothing about any trip. I wonder what's wrong with her? I'm sure it's not her lungs. We've had her examined regularly by the best specialists ever since she was a baby. Do you think she might have had an accident, François?"

Why had he drunk all those cocktails? When he had tried to console her after she had told him the news, he was ashamed of his breath. He was sure that she knew he had been drinking. He was sad. Even before he reached home, he had felt a great weight on his shoulders, a heaviness he could not shake off.

"Eat, my poor François. You can telephone later."

No, he wasn't hungry. He had gone downstairs to telephone from the Italian place, even though she had told him Enrico had already tried. If he had come home on time, Enrico would not have had to stick his nose into other people's business.

Enrico had been right.

"All flights to Mexico City are booked solid for ten days," Combe had said when he came back upstairs. "There's a train at seven-thirty in the morning."

"I'll take it."

"Then I'll try to get you Pullman accommodations."

He went back downstairs to telephone. It was raining. The world was gray. The world was oppressive. His movements seemed unreal. He first telephoned the wrong station, of course. American railways mystified him.

The rain was coming down straight and hard, spattering noisily on the sidewalk. He dripped water on the stairs. When he bent his head to thrust his key into his door, water streamed from his hatbrim. Why did such ridiculous details affect him?

"There are no berths left on the morning train, but they told me if you come to the station half an hour before train time, there might be a cancellation."

"I'm putting you to so much trouble, François."

He studied her face carefully. Could it be that her forlorn expression was not due entirely to worry over her daughter? Wasn't Kay also thinking of them, and that they would be separated in a few hours?

There was calamity in that telegram, an evil destiny, in that piece of yellow paper, that seemed the logical sequel to Laugier's lectures and the thoughts that had been running through Combe's head ever since. A man was tempted to believe that there was no escape, that Destiny would take care of putting things in order. The most disturbing thought was that he was almost resigned to whatever might happen. It was very depressing, this sudden weakness, this absolute lack of any reaction on his part.

She was packing. She said: "I don't know what to do about money. The banks were already closed when Enrico came. I could take a later train, maybe."

"There's none before evening."

"Enrico wanted to— Now, don't be angry. Nothing really matters right now, you know. He told me that if I needed money, any amount, I could call him at home, even at night. I didn't know if you—"

"Could you get along with four hundred dollars?"

"Of course, François. Only . . ." They never talked about money.

"I can spare it. Truly."

"Maybe I could give you a note or something, I don't know, that you could take to the bank tomorrow and they would give you the money instead of me."

"We can wait until you get back." He spoke as if he really believed that she was coming back, but he didn't look at her. He was afraid that she might not believe what he was saying.

"You'll have to get some sleep, Kay."

"I couldn't."

"Go to bed."

"Do you think it's worth while? It's already two o'clock, and I'll have to leave here by six, in case we don't get a taxi right away. So that means I'll have to get up at five," she went on. "You want me to have a cup of coffee, don't you?"

She lay down on the bed, fully dressed. He walked around for a moment, then lay down beside her. They didn't speak. They didn't close their eyes. They stared at the ceiling.

He had never in his life felt so depressed, so darkly desperate. It was a despair without words, without precise subject. It was a feeling of desolation against which there was no defense. He whispered in her ear, "Will you come back?"

For an answer she sought his hand and squeezed it for a long moment.

"I wish I could die in her place."

"Stop it. Nobody's going to die." He wondered if she was crying. He touched her eyelids. They were dry.

"You'll be all alone, François. That's what hurts me

the most. Tomorrow, when you come home from the station—"

She sat up suddenly, her eyes wide as she looked at François in alarm. "You are taking me to the station, aren't you? You must! Forgive me for insisting, but I don't think I could go through with it alone. I know I must go, but you must send me, even if—"

She fell back again and hid her face in the pillow. They withdrew once more into silence, each wrapped in his own thoughts, rehearsing for the new loneliness they were both to face. . . .

She slept a little. He dozed off in a series of cat naps. He arose first to make the coffee.

At five in the morning the sky was even darker than it was at midnight, and the street lights seemed unable to dispel the gloom. The rain continued to spatter down with a determination that promised to last all day.

"Time to get up, Kay."

"All right."

He didn't kiss her. They had not exchanged one kiss all night, perhaps because of Michèle, perhaps because each was afraid of breaking down.

"Dress warmly."

"I've nothing warmer than my fur."

"Wear a wool dress, anyhow."

They managed to keep the conversation confined to the commonplace.

"Trains are always overheated, you know."

She drank her coffee but couldn't eat anything. He helped her close her suitcase, which was too full. She looked around the room as she said, "Do you mind if I leave the rest of my things here?"

"It's time to go. Come on."

133

There were only two lighted windows in the whole street. More people catching an early train? Sickness?

"You stand in the doorway. I'll see if I can find a cab."

"We'll lose time."

"If I don't find one right away, we'll take the subway. You'll stay here, won't you?"

What a stupid question! Where would she go? He turned up the collar of his topcoat, ducked his head against the rain, and, hugging the buildings, ran for the corner. He had scarcely reached it when he heard her voice behind him:

"François! François!"

Kay stood in the middle of the sidewalk, gesticulating. A taxi had stopped two doors away, bringing a couple home from a night out. The night shift going off, so to speak; the day shift going on. Kay held the cab door open and spoke to the driver while Combe went after her suitcase.

"Pennsylvania Station."

The seat was damp and sticky. Everything was wet around them. The air was raw. She snuggled against him. Neither of them spoke as they rode through the deserted streets.

"Don't get out, François," she said when they reached the station. "Go on home."

She bore down on the word *home* to give him courage.

"You have an hour to wait."

"It doesn't matter. I'll get something warm to drink. I'll try to eat a little."

She tried to smile, but she made no effort to get out.

"I mean it, François. Don't come any farther."

It wasn't cowardice on his part. He actually did not have the strength to follow her into the labyrinth of the station, to sit watching the huge hand of the monumental clock jump away the minutes, to live out the final seconds

134

of their separation, to be caught up in the crowd surging forward when the gates were opened, to see her climb aboard the train that would carry her off.

She bent over him. There were raindrops on her fur. Her lips were burning hot. They clung to each other for a long moment, oblivious of the driver. He saw the glow in her eyes, heard her stammering as though in a dream:

"Now I don't feel any more that I'm going away. It's more like coming home, darling."

She broke away from him, opened the door, signaled a redcap to take her suitcase. She took three quick steps, stopped and turned. She was pale, but she was smiling.

She held her bag in one hand. She raised the other, but not very high, no higher than the elbow. She waved good-by with her fingers. Then she was swallowed up by the glass door.

He watched her through the glass, trotting off behind the redcap, a picture he would remember always. . . .

"Where to now, bud?" The taxi driver had turned around to break into his mood.

He gave his address. Automatically he filled his pipe. His mouth was fuzzy from his sleepless night.

She had said, ". . . like coming home . . ."

He sensed a vague promise.

But he still hadn't quite understood.

chapter 8

Kay dear,

I know Enrico has told you what happened to me, so you know that Ronald has really been very nice about it all, every inch the gentleman. He has preserved his usual calm which you know so well, and has not even gone into one of his cold furies which are his specialty. I don't know what would have happened if he had, in view of the state I was in . . .

Combe had not taken the nose dive he expected. Instead it had been a slow sinking, day by day, hour by hour, into the quicksands of solitude. During the first days he had even acted as a fairly reasonable human being. He had been borne up by the hope generated during the interminable hours of that very short final night.

"Will you telephone me?" It was a plea.

137

"Here?"

He had sworn that he would have a phone installed before she got to Mexico, and he had gone to work immediately, for fear that she might call before he had a number. After all, in France it sometimes took months.

"Will you telephone?"

"Of course, darling. If I can."

"You can if you really want to."

"I'll phone you."

The formalities had been simple, so simple that he was almost annoyed. He had expected a complex, world-shaking operation. And his phone was installed the day after he had made application. After that, he was afraid to leave the house, even though Kay had probably not yet reached Mexico City.

"I'll call information in New York," she had said. "They'll give me your number."

He himself called information several times a day to make sure they were aware that he was now a subscriber and that they could furnish his number on request.

He didn't want to go out anyhow. Life was gray and grimy. The city was gray and grimy. The rain had turned into melted snow. The streets were so dark he could hardly see the little tailor in his cell of the honeycomb across the street.

Kay seemed to have dissolved in the rain and snow. All he could remember of her now was the last glimpse he had of her through the glass panel of the door at the railway station—a blurred, receding image he clung to desperately. . . .

Letters came for her, forwarded from Jessie's address.

"Open them all," she had said. "I have no secrets from you, as you well know."

Still, he had hesitated. It was not until there were half

a dozen of them, and he noted one envelope bearing the house flag of the Grace Line. It was a letter from Jessie, air-mailed from somewhere in the Caribbean.

. . . in view of the state I was in . . .

He knew them all by heart now.

. . . if I hadn't wanted to avoid a scene, at all costs . . .

It was all so far away. He had the impression of watching a scene in a topsy-turvy world through the wrong end of a telescope.

> *I know very well that if Ric were driven into a corner, he would have left his wife without hesitation. . . .*

He repeated it to himself: driven into a corner!

> *. . . but I chose to go away. It's going to be painful. And it will probably be long. This is a difficult moment to live through. How happy we were together, my poor Kay, in our little apartment!*
>
> *I wonder if those days will ever come back. I don't dare hope so. Ronald chills me and puzzles me, and yet there's nothing I can reproach him for. Instead of those terrible rages he used to go into sometimes, he's so calm that he scares me. He doesn't leave me for a minute. I sometimes feel that he's trying to read my mind.*
>
> *And he's so sweet, so considerate, more than he ever was before, even on our honeymoon. Do you remember the story of the pineapple that made you laugh so hard? Well, that could never happen again now.*

*Everybody on board thinks we're newlyweds,
and sometimes it's funny. Yesterday we changed
from woolens to linens because we're getting into
the tropics. It's getting very warm. It seemed
strange to see everybody in white all of a sudden,
even the officers. There's one young officer (he
has only one stripe) who can't keep his sheep's
eyes off of me. Don't mention this to Ric, please;
he might go into a decline.*

*I don't know how things are with you back
there, my poor Kay, but I imagine they must be
pretty awful. I can put myself in your place. I can
picture your confusion and only hope you are
making out somehow. . . .*

It was a strange sensation. There were times when he
could see the world without shadows, without clouds,
lucidly, objectively, in such raw, harsh colors that after a
while he felt physical pain.

My dear Kay:

This letter came in an envelope bearing a French
stamp and a Toulon postmark. Hadn't Kay told him to
open them all?

*I haven't heard from you for nearly five months
now, but I'm not too surprised. . . .*

He read slowly, to get the full meaning of every word.

*I found a rather disagreeable surprise waiting
for me when we got back to France. My sub-
marine had been transferred from the Atlantic to
the Mediterranean Fleet. In other words, my
home port was to be Toulon instead of our good
old Brest. It wasn't so bad for me, but for my*

wife, who had just rented a new villa and had barely finished getting settled, it was such a disappointment that she fell ill. . . .

This was obviously the man who had slept with Kay. Combe knew it; he knew where and under what circumstances. He knew all the details. Hadn't he practically begged for them? He was hurt and he was pleased at the same time.

We're settled now in La Seyne, a not too pleasant suburb. But there's a streetcar that takes me right to the port and there's a park across the street where the children can play.

That's right, he had children too.

Chubby is fine and getting fatter than ever. He sends his regards.

Chubby!

Fernand is no longer with us. He has been assigned to the Naval Ministry in Paris, which is just the place for him. He's always had an air of high society about him, and he'll fit in very well with the parties on Rue Royale. As for your friend Riri, all I can say is that we have not spoken to each other, except in the line of duty, since we left the shores of wonderful America. I don't know whether he's jealous of me or I of him. He probably doesn't know either. It's up to you, my little Kay, to settle the argument. . . .

He sank his fingernails into the palms of his hands, yet he was quite calm. He was so calm during those first days that he sometimes mistook the void he was living in as the irrevocable void. At such times he would tell himself, *It's all over*.

He was free again, free to drop in at the Ritz Bar any evening he liked at six, drink as many cocktails as he wanted with Laugier, talk all night if he felt like it. And if Laugier asked about his "mouse," he was also free to say, "What mouse?"

No doubt about it, he sometimes felt a certain relief. Laugier was right. This affair was bound to turn out badly. In any event, it could not turn out well. There were times when he wanted to see Laugier again. On several occasions he got as far as the entrance to the Ritz, but his guilt feelings never let him go into the bar.

Other mail came for Kay, mostly bills. There was a bill from the cleaner and one from a milliner who had done something to her hat, probably the hat she wore on the night they first met. He could see it now, perched over one eye, and the bill immediately assumed a sentimental value.

One dollar twenty-nine cents . . .

Not for the hat, but for doing something to the trimming—adding or subtracting a ribbon or some other silly feminine trifle.

One dollar twenty-nine cents . . .

He remembered the figure. He remembered too that the milliner was located on 260th Street. It was a long way to go, far up in the Bronx, and he pictured Kay walking there, the way they had trudged up and down Fifth Avenue together at night. They had certainly done a lot of walking. . . .

Nobody had called him since his phone was installed, not surprising in as much as nobody but Kay knew that he had one. Kay had promised, "I'll call you as soon as I can."

142

But Kay had not called. He was almost afraid to go out, just in case the phone should ring while he was gone. For hours he would sit as though hypnotized, watching the bearded tailor across the street. He knew the routine of his life by heart—at what time he ate, at what time he assumed his sacerdotal pose, and what time he got down from his workbench. Solitude studying solitude.

He was almost ashamed of the capon that Kay had insisted on sending the old man. He could put himself in the other's place. . . .

My dear little Kay . . .

Everybody called her Kay. It made him furious. Why had she told him to open all her letters?

This one was in English, rather stiff and formal.

> *I received your letter of August 14 and was glad to learn that you were in the country. I hope that the Connecticut air has done you some good. I myself was unable to get away from New York for as long as I wanted because my business kept me tied down. However . . .*

However what? This one too had slept with her. They had all slept with her. Would he never get rid of that nightmare?

> *. . . my wife would be delighted if you . . .*

The bastard! No, he wasn't a bastard. It was Combe who was wrong. But he didn't have to be wrong any longer, since it was all over. All he had to do was write, "Finished," period. Period, new paragraph. That was all he needed to end his suffering. Otherwise he would be suffering on her account until the end of his days.

That much was definite. He would suffer on her account to the end of his days.

And he was resigned to it.

Stupidly.

What would an imbecile like Laugier say if he confessed such a conclusion?

It was very simple, however, so simple that . . . Well, he could find no words for it. That's the way it was. Kay wasn't there and he needed Kay. He had seen himself as a tragic figure once because his wife, at the age of forty, wanted to experience a new love and feel young again. How childish he had been! Had it been of the slightest importance?

He knew now that it had not. The only thing that mattered now, the only thing in the world that was important, was Kay—Kay and her past, Kay and . . .

Kay and a phone call. That was all, just a phone call. He waited all day and all night. He set the alarm for one in the morning, to make sure he would not sleep through the first few rings and that the operator might stop ringing. Then he set the alarm for two, then three.

When the telephone persisted in its maddening silence, he would say to himself, *Good. Fine. It's all over. It couldn't end in any other way.* For he had the taste of catastrophe on his lips.

No, it couldn't end in any other way. He would be himself again, François Combe. They would welcome him at the Ritz like a man recovering from a serious operation.

"Well, is it over?"

"All over."

"It didn't hurt too much? Are you still sore?"

And there was no one there at night to hear him begging his pillow:

"Kay, my little Kay, please telephone me. Please!"

The streets were empty. New York was empty. Even their little bar was empty. One day he went there for a drink and to bribe the jukebox to play their song, but he could not listen to it because a drunken Scandinavian sailor insisted on clinging to him while pouring out unintelligible secrets.

Wasn't it better this way? She was gone for good. She had known that she was going for good. They had both known it would be forever.

I don't feel any more that I'm going away . . . It's more like coming home, darling. . . .

What had she meant by that? Why was it like coming home? Home to whom?

Dear Madam: You have probably overlooked our bill for . . .

Three dollars and some cents. For a shirtwaist that he remembered having taken from Jessie's closet and handed to Kay, who was packing.

Kay was Kay—a menace to his peace of mind and to his future. Kay was Kay, whom he could no longer do without. He would reject her ten times a day, only to ask forgiveness ten times—to reject her again a few minutes later. And he avoided all contact with men, as though they were dangerous. He had not returned to the studio. He had seen neither Hourvitch nor Laugier. He disliked them heartily.

Finally on the seventh day, or rather the seventh night, while he was fast asleep, the telephone bell shattered the silence of his apartment. The alarm clock stood beside the instrument. It was two in the morning.

"Hello." He could hear the long-distance operators exchanging service messages. One of them repeated stupidly, "Hello, Mr. Combe . . . ? Mr. Combe . . . ? I have a long-distance call for Mr. Combe, C—O—M—B—E."

"Hello . . . this is Combe." In the background he

thought that he could hear Kay's voice saying hello, but she had not yet been put through.

"Mr. François Combe?"

"Yes, speaking."

"Just a moment. Go ahead, Mexico."

She was there, at the other end of the night. She asked softly:

"Is that you?"

And he found nothing better to say than:

"Is that you?"

He had told her once—and she had laughed—that she had two voices: one was the commonplace, undistinguished voice of any woman; the other was deeper, a little husky, which he had loved the first time he had heard it.

He had never before heard her voice over the telephone and was delighted to find that it was the deeper one, a little lower-pitched than he remembered, warmer, with just a hint of a tenderly seductive drawl. He wanted to shout, *You know, Kay, I've given up. I'm not fighting it any longer.* He was eager to tell her the news, because he had just found it out a few seconds earlier.

"I couldn't call you any sooner," she was saying. "I'll tell you all about it later. But everything seems to be all right here. Michèle is getting the best of care. Only it has been very hard to telephone. It still is. But from now on I'm going to try every night."

"Can't I call you? At what hotel are you staying?"

There was a pause.

"François, I've had to move into the embassy, but don't imagine things, please. Nothing has changed, I swear. When I got here, Michèle had just been operated on. It was an emergency. It was critical. Acute appendicitis. And then peritonitis developed. Can you hear me?"

146

"Certainly. Who were you talking to?"

"The maid. A nice old Mexican woman, God bless her, who has a room on my floor. She heard me talking and she wondered if I needed something."

He heard Spanish spoken in the background.

"Darling, are you still there? To go on with Michèle. She's had the best surgeons in the country. The operation was successful. But there is always the danger of complications for a few days. And that's that, my little sweetheart."

My little sweetheart! She had never called him that before. It was a depressing term of endearment.

"I think of you all the time, you know. I worry about you, all alone in your little apartment. Are you very unhappy?"

"I don't know. Yes. No . . ."

"You sound so funny."

"Really? That's because you've never heard my voice on the telephone before. When are you coming back?"

"I don't know yet. As soon as I can, I promise. Maybe in three or four days."

"That's a long time."

"What, darling?"

"I said, that's an awfully long time."

She laughed. At least he thought he heard her laughing.

"I'm in my nightgown and my bathrobe, and I'm standing barefoot, because the telephone is near the fireplace and it's quite chilly tonight. Are you in bed?"

Where did she think he was? He said nothing. He had been looking forward with such enthusiasm to this call that now he hardly recognized her voice.

"Have you been a good boy, François?"

He said he had. Then he heard her humming, thou-

147

sands of miles away at the other end of the line, so softly he could hardly hear her—their song.

Something warm surged up inside him, something that flooded his breast and welled up into his throat. He couldn't breathe, he couldn't open his mouth. Then the humming stopped, and there was a moment of silence. He wondered if she was crying, whether she too was speechless. Then she said:

"Good night, my François. Sleep well. I'll call you tomorrow. Good night."

There was a faint sound that might have been a kiss winging its way from halfway to the equator. He must have stammered something that nobody understood. The operator was saying something he could not understand, something like "Your three minutes are up . . ."

"Good night."

That was all he could say. His bed was terribly empty.

"Good night, my François."

He hadn't told her what he wanted to tell her. He hadn't given her the all-important news that had been screaming to be told. Only after he had hung up did the words form on his lips. *You know, Kay? . . . What, my sweetheart? . . . What you told me at the station. The last thing you said . . . Yes, my sweetheart . . . That you didn't feel as if you were going away . . . that you were coming home? . . .*

She would have been smiling, far away at the other end of the line, a million miles away. He could see her smiling, while he spoke aloud in the void of his lonely room.

I know what you mean now, finally. It's taken me a long time, hasn't it? But you mustn't be angry with me.

No, my sweetheart.

148

Because men, you know, are a little obtuse. And then there's always that masculine pride. . . .

Yes, my sweetheart. It doesn't matter.

You got home first, but I'm with you now. We've both come home, haven't we. And isn't it wonderful?

Wonderful, my sweetheart.

Don't cry. You mustn't cry. I'm not crying either. But I haven't got used to this yet. Do you understand?

I understand.

But it's all over now. It's been a long, hard road, but I've come home at last. And I know now. I love you. Do you hear me, Kay? I love you . . . I love you . . . I love you!

He buried his damp, salty face in his pillow. His body was racked with sobs. Far, far away he could see Kay smiling at him. He could even hear her warmer, deeper voice murmuring in his ear, *Yes, my sweetheart.*

chapter 9

A letter came for him in the morning mail. Even without the Mexican stamp he would have known that it was from Kay. He had never seen her handwriting before, but it was the very essence of Kay, so much so that he was moved by merely looking at it. This was a Kay that, he was certain, nobody else knew—a somewhat childish Kay, at once timorous and terribly reckless.

He was probably being ridiculous, but he thought that he could imagine the curves of her body in the curves of certain letters. The very fine downstrokes were like the almost invisible lines in her face. There were sudden, unexpected marks of boldness, and there were signs of physical weakness. A skilled graphologist would doubtless discover marks of her illness in her hand, for Combe was convinced that she had never been completely cured, that she would carry her wounds with her all her life. . . . He smiled at

151

her retracings when she stumbled over a difficult word or was not sure of the spelling.

She had not mentioned the letter during her telephone call. She had so many other things to talk about she had probably forgotten all about it.

The monotonous gray of the city became, that morning, a soft, tender dove gray. The continuous patter of the rain made a muted obbligato to his thoughts as he read:

My great big darling,

How alone and unhappy you must be! I've been here for three days now and I have found no time to write or a way to telephone. But I have never stopped thinking of my poor François, who must be worrying back there in New York.

I'm sure that you feel lost and abandoned, and I still wonder what I could have done, what you can possibly see in me that has made my presence so necessary to you. If only you could have seen how miserable you looked when our taxi reached the station. It took all the courage I had to keep from turning around and coming back to you. May I confess, though, that it made me very happy?

Perhaps I shouldn't tell you this, but you are never out of my thoughts, even when I'm with my daughter.

I'll telephone you tonight or tomorrow night, depending on how my daughter is getting along, for I've spent every night at the hospital since my arrival. They put up a cot for me in a room next to Michèle's. Since the door is always open, I haven't dared put in a call for New York, and I admit I'm afraid to call from the office because the vixen with glasses who runs it doesn't like me. If all goes well, this will be my last night at the hospital.

But I must hurry and tell you everything in detail, for I know that otherwise you will imagine all sorts of things, just to torture yourself. First of all, I must confess right away that I almost deceived you. But not in the way you think, my poor dear, as you will see in a minute. After I left you in the taxi and bought my ticket, I suddenly felt so forlorn that I rushed for the snack bar. I wanted so terribly to cry, my poor François! I could still see your face looking out through the taxi window, haggard and tragic.

There was a man next to me at the lunch counter. I couldn't tell you what he looked like, whether he was young or old. Whoever he was, I said to him:

"Speak to me, will you please? I still have twenty minutes before my train leaves. Say anything at all, anything, so I won't burst into tears right here in public."

He must have thought I was an imbecile. I certainly was acting like one, as usual, I realized afterward. But I had to talk. I had to pour out my heart to somebody, but I don't remember any more what all I told this stranger for the next quarter hour. I talked of you, of us. I told him that I was going away and that you were staying behind. Then I thought that I'd have time to phone you before the train left. I didn't realize, until after I was in the booth, that you had no phone yet.

I wonder how I managed to get aboard the train but I did, and I slept all day. I didn't even have the courage to walk to the dining car. All I had to eat that day was an orange.

Am I boring you with all this? My daughter is asleep. The nurse has just gone out. She takes care of another patient on the floor and has to change an ice bag every hour. I'm in bed in a little white room like I had in the sanatorium, with one small light shining on the writing paper propped against my raised knees.

I think of you and of us. I still wonder how it's possible. I wondered all during the trip. I can't get rid of the feeling, you see, that I don't deserve you. And I'm so afraid of hurting you again. You know what I mean, my François, but I'm convinced now that one day you will realize that this is the first time I have ever been in love. Don't you begin to feel it? I hope so for your sake. I don't want you to be hurt any more.

I must stop writing about these things, or I might pick up the phone and call New York, whether my daughter overhears or not.

I was quite confused to find that Michèle was already quite a young lady. She looks much more like me now than she did when she was small, and everyone insisted that she was the image of her father. She has noticed this too, and she looks at me—forgive me if I seem just a little conceited to write this—she looks at me, as I said, with more than a little admiration.

As my train was not to arrive until nearly midnight, I sent Larski a wire from the border. An embassy car was waiting for me at the station. As we drove across the city, just I and the chauffeur, the chauffeur said, "Madame need not worry about the little girl. She was successfully operated on yesterday, and the doctors say that she is out of danger."

I was glad that Larski didn't come to meet me. He wasn't at the embassy, either. I was greeted by a sort of governess, very Hungarian and very much the great-lady-who-has-fallen-upon-unhappy-days. She showed me to the apartment I was to occupy and said, "If you would like to go to the hospital tonight, an embassy car will be at your disposal."

Can you imagine my state of mind, my sweetheart, all alone in that huge palace with just my poor little suitcase?

154

"The maid will draw your bath, after which you will no doubt wish to eat something, perhaps?"

I don't know what I ate. They rolled the table into my room, all set, like in a hotel. They also brought me a bottle of tokay and I must confess (you can either laugh or scold me) that I drank it all.

The hospital was on a hill at the edge of town. Everything was quite formal. L. was in the waiting room with one of the surgeons who had just examined Michèle. He bowed and introduced me to the surgeon:

"The mother of my daughter."

He was in evening dress, which was not unusual for him; he had obviously just come from some diplomatic function; but it made him look more glacial than ever.

The doctor told me that while he was practically sure the crisis was past, the next three or four days would have to be carefully watched. Then he left me alone with L. in a sort of sitting room that reminded me of the reception room of a convent. L., as calm and poised as ever, gave me the details.

"I hope you were not annoyed by the slight delay in my notifying you about Michèle," he said, "but I had some trouble in getting your last address."

And you of course know, my darling, that it was not my last address, because I was already at our place. Forgive me for underlining those two words, but I have to write them, and I say them aloud to convince myself that it's true. I've been unhappy here, but I shouldn't tell you about it because you too are unhappy, and I should be with you. I know that's where I belong.

I'm trying to tell you everything that happened, but my ideas get a little mixed up. Do you know that I don't even know how long Michèle has been in

155

Mexico? We haven't talked much. She's so intimidated by my presence that she hardly opens her mouth. And when I start asking questions, the nurse breaks in to tell me I mustn't tire the patient.

What was I saying, François? I've forgotten how many days I have been here. I sleep in the room next to Michèle's, as I told you, and she often talks in her sleep, almost always in Hungarian. She mentions names I have never heard before. In the morning I help the nurse with her toilet. Her little body reminds me of mine when I was her age, and makes me want to cry. She's just as modest and bashful as I was then. For part of her ablutions she won't even let me stay in the room, not even if I turn my back.

I don't know what she thinks of me or what people have told her about me. She looks at me curiously and with some astonishment. When her father comes, she looks at us both in silence.

And I, François, think of you all the time, even—and this is not a nice thing to write—even the other evening, about ten o'clock, when Michèle fainted and scared everyone so that they telephoned the opera to have her father paged. Am I a heartless monster?

L. too looks at me with some astonishment. I sometimes wonder if something hasn't changed in me since I've known you and loved you, something that strikes even people who don't know me. You should see the looks I get from the dowager governess of the embassy. . . .

Every morning the car comes to the hospital to take me back to the embassy. I go up to my apartment and have my meals there. I have never seen the great dining hall. And the only glimpse I have had of the magnificent reception rooms was one morning when the cleaning women were in one of them and had left the doors open.

I have had only one real conversation with L. He telephoned me one day to ask if I could come to his office in the chancellery at eleven in the morning. Like all the others, he looked me over with some surprise. There may have been just a hint of pity in his expression, too; he could hardly fail to notice that my wardrobe is a little shabby, that I wear no jewelry, and that I have not bothered to use make-up since I have been here. But there is no getting around the fact that there was more than pity in his eyes. I don't know what it is and I can't explain it, but there is no doubt that being in love somehow gets through to people in a vague and confused manner, and the impression makes them feel ill at ease.

He asked me, "Are you happy?"

I said yes so simply, while looking him straight in the eyes, that he was the first to look away.

"I am taking advantage, if that is the phrase," he said, "of the occasion that has thrown us together again accidentally, to inform you of my forthcoming marriage."

"I thought you had already remarried."

"I had. It was a mistake." He disposed of the matter with a wave of his hand. Now don't be jealous, François, but he really has very distinguished hands. "This marriage," he continued, "is the final one. I am recommencing my life. That is why I sent for Michèle. She will have her place in my new home."

For a minute I thought I was going to faint. I'm sure I turned pale. I really don't know how I looked at the moment, but I swear—please believe me, darling —that the only thing I could think of was you. I wanted so much to say to him:

"As for me, I'm terribly in love."

But he already knew it. He could feel it. People could not help sensing it.

"And that is why, Catherine," he went on (excuse me once more, darling. I don't want to hurt you, but I must tell you everything), "that is why you must not be vexed because I have excluded you from my daily life here, and why I hope your stay will not be unduly prolonged. I have merely done my duty."

"I am very grateful."

"There are several other matters that I have wanted settled for some time, but if I have not done so, it is only because I had been unable to find your address."

I'll tell you all about it when I see you, François. I have not actually made any hard-and-fast commitments. But please believe that everything I have done I have done for your sake, with you in mind, and in the belief that we will always be together.

Now you know pretty much everything about my life here. You needn't think that I feel any humiliation. I am a stranger in the house. I speak to no one except the governess and the servants. They are polite but distant . . . all except one girl from Budapest. Her name is Nouchi. One morning she surprised me getting out of my bath, and she said, "Madame has skin exactly like Mademoiselle Michèle's."

Do you remember, my darling, the night that you told me that you loved my skin? Well, my daughter's is much softer, much whiter. And her flesh . . .

Here I am getting sentimental again. I swore I would not be sad tonight when I wrote to you. But I would so much like to be able to bring you something worth while! And I bring you nothing. On the contrary. You know what I am thinking about, what you are thinking about all the time, in spite of yourself, and the thought frightens me so that I wonder if I should return to New York. If I were a real heroine, like in the novels, I probably would not come back. I would disappear without leaving any address —and perhaps you would be quickly consoled. But I am not a heroine, my François. You see? I am not even a mother. I lie here in the room next to my daughter, and I think only of my lover, and it is to my lover that I am writing. For the first time in my life, I am proud of writing that word.

My lover!

Like in our song. Do you still remember it? Have you been listening to it? I hope not, because I can see your forlorn face as you listen, and I am afraid you would start drinking too much.

You mustn't. I wonder what you do with your days, your long days of waiting. You must spend hours and hours in our room and by now I'm sure you know every detail in the life of our little tailor. I miss him too. I must stop thinking of New York, or I will find myself risking a scandal and telephoning you right now, come what may. I hope you ran into no delay in having your phone connected.

I still don't know whether Michèle will be well enough tomorrow night or the night after so that I can sleep at the embassy with a clear conscience. There I have a phone in my bedroom. I've already said to L. in an offhand way, "Will you mind if I have to make a phone call to New York?"

I could see his jaws tighten. Now don't start imagining things, darling. It's an old tic of his. It's about the only sign of emotion I've ever been able to discover in his face. I think he would have been quite happy to find that I was alone in the world, a castaway, even. Not for his own advantage, though.

That's all over and done with. But to satisfy his own wounded vanity, which is incredible.

He bowed from the waist—another of his mannerisms he thinks is the mark of a great diplomat—and replied coldly:

"Whenever you wish."

He knew what kind of call I wanted to make, and I, my darling, was dying to put a name to his suspicion. I wanted to shout in his face, "François!"

If I'm to stay here much longer, I'll have to find somebody who'll listen to me talk about you, anybody, like at the railway station. You're not angry with me, are you, because of that silly business at the station? It was only because of you, darling—I simply couldn't keep you shut up inside of me any longer.

I can still see the expression on your face the night you said to me, "You just can't help turning on the charm, can you, even if it's just for the bus boy in a cafeteria or a taxi driver? You are so hungry for the admiration of men that you expect it even from the beggar you give a dime to in the street."

Well, I'm going to confess something else. No, I'd better not; you wouldn't understand. And yet . . . what if you don't? What if I told you that I almost told my daughter about you? In fact, I did mention you vaguely—oh, very vaguely—don't worry—as though I was talking to an old and trusted friend. . . .

It's already four o'clock in the morning. I had no idea it was so late. I've run out of paper. I've already written in all the margins, as you can see. I hope you won't have too much trouble deciphering this.

I want so much for you not to be sad, or too lonely. I want you, too, to have confidence in us. I would give anything to prevent your being hurt any more on my account.

Tomorrow night or the night after I will telephone you. I will hear your voice, and I will be with you—in our home.

I am exhausted.

Good night, François.

He radiated so much genuine happiness next day he was sure that anyone coming near him must feel its warmth.

It was so simple. So simple!

And so simply beautiful!

Some of the old pain persisted, like the dull twinges of convalescence, but they were lost in the great serenity that enveloped him.

She would come back, and life would begin again. That was all. He repeated it over and over to himself: *She'll come back. She's coming back and life will start over*.

He had no urge to dance with joy, to laugh, or even to smile. He took his happiness with calm and dignity. And he was not going to give way to his doubts. Ridiculous little doubts, weren't they?

This letter was written three days ago. Much can happen in three days. Who knows if . . . ?

Just as his imagination had tried to re-create—inaccurately—the apartment she had shared with Jessie before he had seen it, so he now tried to conjure up a picture of the vast Hungarian Embassy in Mexico City, and of Larski, whom he had never seen. He could see Larski sitting across his ambassadorial desk from Kay, making this proposal she had accepted without really accepting it, and that she had postponed explaining.

Would she telephone him again tonight? At what time?

She must telephone, because he had something important to tell her. He had been so stupidly tongue-tied on the phone that she knew nothing of what had been going on inside him. She still did not know that he was in love with her. How could she know, since he himself had not known until a few hours ago?

So? What was going to happen next? Perhaps they would no longer be tuned in on the same wave length when they met again. At any rate, he must tell her the big news. Since her daughter was out of danger, why didn't she come right home? Why was she dawdling down there anyhow, surrounded by hostile influences? And what about that silly idea of hers—disappearing without a trace, just because she had hurt him and would go on hurting him?

No, no! He must explain to her that everything was different now. He had to get through to her. She must be told. Otherwise she might do something stupidly rash.

His happiness suddenly became only potential happiness, like a promissory note payable in the future but on which the interest payments would be days of anxiety. He was terribly afraid now that he had lost his chance. He would tell her to hurry back by plane.

But suppose the plane should crash? He would tell her to return by train. Still, the train took days instead of hours. And trains, too, could be wrecked.

They would talk it over when she phoned. And since she said that she would not telephone before night, he could go out for a while.

Laugier had been idiotic. Worse. He had been perfidious. His long lecture the other evening had been nothing short of perfidy. Because Laugier too must have felt what Kay had been writing about—the aura of love, which infuriates people who are not in love.

In a pinch we might get her a job as usherette in a movie theater. . . .

162

Those weren't his exact words, but that was his plan for Kay.

Combe did not have a glass of wine all day. He did not want to drink. He wanted to enjoy his new-found calm and tranquillity because, in spite of everything, he was enjoying tranquillity. It was not before six in the evening that he made up his mind—although he knew all along that he was going to do it—to go and see Laugier at the Ritz Bar, not so much to annoy him as to display his peace of mind.

Perhaps if Laugier had teased him, as he had expected, or even if he had shown himself a trifle more aggressive, things might have turned out differently. Laugier was holding court at his usual table, surrounded by his usual crowd, including the American girl Combe had met before.

"How are things, old boy?" Laugier shook hands, perhaps a little more cordially than usual, and his expression seemed to say, *See? That's done it. What did I tell you?*

Did the idiot imagine that it was all washed up, that he had thrown Kay over? They wouldn't mention the subject again. The affair had been liquidated. Combe was once more a normal male. . . . Did they really think that?

Well, Combe didn't want to be a normal male at the moment. He had an urge to give them all a pitying look. He suddenly missed Kay so much that a wave of dizziness swept over him. Was it possible that no one saw a change in him? Or was he really normal, like the others around him, the people for whom he felt only disdain?

He acted normally. He drank a manhattan, accepted a second, and talked to the American girl who was ringing a cigarette with lipstick as she asked him (in French) about the plays he had starred in, in Paris.

He had a desperate, almost painful need of Kay's physical presence at that moment, and yet he was behaving like

163

a normal male. He was a little surprised at himself, spreading his reputation like a peacock his tail, as he boasted, with perhaps more spirit than it deserved, of his stage career.

Rat-face was not there. Other people he had not met before claimed to have seen his films.

He wanted to talk of Kay. He had her letter in his pocket and at times he was ready to take it out and read it to whoever would listen—the American girl, for instance, whom he had hardly noticed the week before. *They don't know. They can't know.*

He drank his cocktails automatically as they were served. He thought: *Three more days. Four at most. She'll telephone me again tonight, and she'll hum our song.* He was in love with Kay, no doubt about it. He had never loved her as much as he did that night. And that very night he was going to discover a new shape of their love, perhaps its very roots.

But the present was still confused and would always remain confused, like a bad dream. For instance, the self-satisfied smile on Laugier's lips and the little spark of irony in his eyes. Why was Laugier suddenly making fun of him? Because he was talking to the American girl? Well, he would go on talking to the American girl—about Kay. She had given him his cue.

"You're married, aren't you?" she had asked. "Is your wife with you in New York?"

And he had told her about Kay. He told her that he had come to New York alone and that loneliness had made him understand the inestimable value of a human relationship. His body as well as his spirit had ached with loneliness. He had met Kay. They had at once plunged as deeply into the intimacy of their beings as human nature would allow. Because they were starved for human contact.

The words seemed suddenly so heavy with meaning, there in the crowded, smoky din of the Ritz Bar, that they were like a revelation. He emptied his glass. Human contact!

"You wouldn't understand, of course," he said. "How could you understand?"

There was Laugier smiling cynically at him from the next table, where he was talking with a producer!

Combe was sincere. He spoke ardently. He was full of Kay, full to overflowing. He remembered the first time they had fallen into each other's arms, knowing nothing about one another except that they were both starved for human contact.

He repeated the phrase, tried to find its equivalent in English. The American girl watched him with eyes that grew pensive.

"She'll be in New York in three or four days," he said. "Maybe sooner, if she gets a seat on a plane."

"How happy she must be!"

Time had slipped by. The bar was emptying. Laugier got up and held out his hand.

"I must leave you, my children," he said. "By the way, François, will you be a good boy and see June home?"

Combe had the vague feeling that he was the object of a conspiracy, but he was not willing to believe it.

Hadn't Kay given him everything that was possible for a woman to give? Here were two creatures, making their separate ways over the surface of the globe, lost in the great maze of thousands of New York streets. Yet Fate throws them together, and a few hours later they are so fiercely cemented to each other that the very idea of separation is intolerable. Isn't that a miracle? And it was this miracle that he was trying to explain to June, who was watching

165

him with eyes in which he thought he saw a yearning for the new worlds he was opening for her.

"Which way are you going?"

"I don't know. I'm in no hurry."

So he took her to his little bar. He felt that he had to go there that evening, yet he hadn't the courage to go alone.

June too was wearing a fur piece, and she too took his arm. It was a little like having Kay with him. After all, hadn't they been talking of Kay, and only of Kay, all evening?

"Is she very beautiful?"

"No."

"But . . . ?"

"She's very exciting. She is handsome. You would have to see her. She is femininity personified. She is the universal woman, you understand. But I'm sure you don't understand. A woman who is rather sophisticated but who has remained a child. Let's go in here. I want you to hear . . ."

He fumbled in his pocket for nickels. He dropped several in the jukebox, watched June with the hope that she would immediately share *their* emotion.

"Two manhattans, bartender."

He knew he shouldn't go on drinking, but it was too late to stop now. He was so moved by the music that tears came to his eyes. The American girl stroked his hand as if to comfort him. "You shouldn't cry, since she's coming back."

He clenched his fists. "But can't you understand that I can't wait? Three days, four days are an eternity!"

"Shh! People are looking at you."

"I'm sorry."

He fed more nickels to the jukebox—three, four. Every

166

time the record began again, he ordered another round of cocktails.

"At night we would walk up Fifth Avenue for hours." He was tempted to walk up Fifth Avenue with June, just to show her, to make her feel what he had felt. . . .

"I would love to know Kay," she said, staring into space.

"You'll meet her. I want you to know her." He meant it without reservation. "There are so many places in New York now where I can't bear to go to alone."

"I understand." She took his hand again. She seemed to be quite as affected as he was. "Let's go," she said.

Go where? He had no idea of the time, but he certainly didn't want to go home to his lonely cubicle. He had a brain wave. "All right," he said. "I'll take you to a place where Kay and I used to go."

In the taxi she snuggled against him and reached for his hand. Then it seemed to him . . . No, it was difficult to put it into words, but it seemed to him that Kay . . . No, not Kay alone, but all humanity, all the love in the world . . .

He couldn't explain it to June. She wouldn't understand. She leaned her head against his shoulder. He breathed a strange fragrance. . . .

"Promise me that you'll introduce her to me."

"Of course."

They walked into the bar at No. 1 Fifth Avenue. The pianist was still trailing his lazy fingers over the keys. She walked ahead of him with the same instinctive pride of a woman a man is following—just like Kay. She sat down and, like Kay, she pushed her fur back from her shoulders, opened her bag, found a cigarette, fumbled for her lighter. Was she too going to lecture the maître d'hôtel?

At this time of night she began to show traces of

fatigue under her eyes, just like Kay, and her cheeks had begun to sag under her make-up.

"Could you give me a light? My lighter has run out of fluid."

He struck a match. She laughed smoke into his face. A moment later, as she whispered something into his ear, her lips brushed his neck.

"Tell me more about Kay," she said. Then, obviously restless, she got up and added, "Let's go."

Go where? The same question—except that now they had both sensed the answer. They were in Greenwich Village. They were a few steps away from Washington Square. She was clinging to his arm, leaning against him with the limpness of abandon. He could feel her hip against his at every step. . . .

And she was Kay. In spite of everything, it was Kay he was seeking. And it was Kay whose haunches pressed against his, it was even Kay's voice—the low-pitched one— when she spoke, and it was a voice that trembled on the edge of turbulence.

When they came to Combe's house, he stopped. For an instant he stood motionless, his eyes closed. Then, with a gesture that was both gentle and resigned, he took her arm. He did not know whether he was sorrier for her or for himself—or for Kay. He nudged her into the doorway.

She climbed the stairs a few steps ahead of him. She too had a run in her stocking.

"Is it still higher?"

True, she didn't know.

She stopped on the landing, and she didn't look at him. He opened the door and reached for the light switch. She clutched his arm.

"No, please. Don't. Do you mind?"

It took him a few seconds to adjust his eyes after the

precise but anemic light of the city streets. He lived for the moment in his sense of touch—the fur, the smoothness of silk, the warmth of a woman's body, the damp, eager pressure of the lips that sought to mold themselves to his.

He thought, *Kay . . .* !

Then he stopped thinking. They tumbled heavily to the bed.

They lay without speaking, without moving, body to body. Neither slept and each knew the other was awake. Combe's eyes were open, and his cheek almost touched the pale blur of her cheek in the darkness. He could see the faint sheen of perspiration on the outline of her nose. There was nothing to do but wait in silence. . . .

The silence was rudely shattered by the ringing of the phone, a clangor so violent they they both jumped. Flustered, Combe fumbled in the dark, groping for the unfamiliar instrument that had rung only once before. It was June, ironically, who came to his aid by turning on the bedside lamp.

"Hello . . . yes . . ." He did not recognize the sound of his own voice. He stood stupidly in the middle of the floor, naked, holding the receiver in one hand. "François Combe, yes . . ."

He saw June getting out of bed. She whispered, "Do you want me to go?"

What for? Go where? She could hear just as well from the bathroom. He shook his head. She went back to bed, lying on her side. Her hair, fanned out over the pillow, was the same color as Kay's—and in the same place.

"Hello." His throat was tight and dry.

"Is that you, François?"

"Of course, my darling."

"What's the matter?"

"Nothing. Why?"

"I don't know. Your voice sounds funny."

"I woke up with a start." He was ashamed of his lie, ashamed not only of lying to Kay, but of lying to her in the presence of the witness who was watching him from the bed. Why, since she had the tact to offer to leave the room, couldn't she be tactful enough to turn her back to him? She was watching him with one eye, and he stared back at that eye, fascinated.

"I have good news for you, darling. I'm leaving tomorrow, or rather this morning, by plane. I'll be in New York this evening. . . . Hello!"

"Yes."

"Haven't you anything to say? What *is* the matter, François? You're hiding something from me. You've been out with Laugier, haven't you?"

"Yes."

"I'll bet you were drinking."

"Yes."

"I was sure that was it, my poor darling. Why didn't you say so? Will I see you tomorrow, then? I mean, this evening?"

"Yes."

"The embassy got me a seat on the plane. I don't know exactly what time the flight is due in New York, but you can find out by calling the air line. Be sure you call the right one, though, because there are several. I'm flying Pan-American."

"Yes." There were so many things he had wanted to tell her. He had wanted most of all to shout out the great news. And instead he stood there dumbly, as though hypnotized by one eye.

"Did you get my letter?"

"This morning."

"Did I make many mistakes in spelling? Did you have the courage to read it right through to the end? You know, I don't think I'll go to bed tonight, although it won't take me long to pack. I went out for an hour this afternoon, and I bought you a present. A surprise. But I'm keeping you up, darling. I can tell you're sleepy. Did you really have a lot to drink?"

"I guess so."

"Was Laugier very disagreeable?"

"I don't really remember, darling. All I know is that I was thinking of you all the time."

"See you this evening, François."

"See you this evening." He wanted to tell her. He tried, but it wouldn't come out. He should have tried harder. He should have confessed, *Listen, Kay, I've got somebody in the room. You understand now why I* . . . He would tell her when she got back. It must not be an act of treachery. There must never be anything underhanded between them.

"Go right to sleep."

"Good night, Kay."

Slowly he replaced the phone in its cradle. For a long moment he stood in the middle of the room, arms dangling, staring at the floor.

"Did she guess?"

"I don't know."

"Will you tell her?"

He raised his head, looked her squarely in the eyes, and said, "Yes."

She was lying on her back, her erect breasts like twin pomegranates. After a while she sat up and tried to straighten her hair. Then she swung her legs off the bed, one after the other, and reached for her stockings.

He made no move to stop her. He too began dressing.

She said without bitterness, "You don't have to see me home. I'll find my way."

"I'll take you home."

"It's better that you shouldn't. She might telephone again."

"You think so?"

"If she suspects something, she'll call you back."

"Please forgive me."

"For what?"

"Nothing. For letting you go alone like this."

"It's my fault."

She smiled. When she had finished dressing, she lit a cigarette. She came up to him and planted a light, sisterly kiss on his forehead. Her fingers sought his and squeezed them warmly as she murmured, "Good luck."

He listened to her footsteps in the stairway. Then he sat down, half dressed, to wait out the night. Kay did not telephone again. The light went on in the little tailor's window across the street, announcing the start of a new day.

Was Combe wrong? Would it always be like this? Would he go on indefinitely discovering new depths of love to be attained? Not a muscle in his face moved. He was stiff and weary in body and mind. He did not feel capable of thought. But he had the conviction—it was a certainty that he felt with all his being—that it was only this night that he had loved Kay truly and totally; at least that he had been so truly and totally aware of it.

That was why, when dawn touched his windows and dimmed the lamp on his night table, he was no longer ashamed of what had happened.

chapter **10**

She wouldn't understand. How could she? She couldn't know, for instance, that during the hour he had been waiting at the airport he had been wondering whether, without any romantic exaggeration, considering the state of his nerves, he would be able to withstand the shock.

Everything he had done that day, everything he had done up to the present moment, would be so radically new to her that he would, in a way, have to start training her all over again. And the burning question was whether they were still on the same wave length, and if so, whether she could and would travel so far with him.

Worrying about this new development had kept him from doing the many things he had planned to do that morning. He had not bothered to change the pillow slip on which June's head had lain; he had not even looked to see if she had left traces of lipstick. What was the use? He was so far beyond all that. It was all in the past.

He had not ordered dinner delivered from the Italian's, as he had been planning. He had not checked the refrigerator to see what there was to eat and drink.

She would never guess what he had actually been doing that day. He had drawn back the drapes and pulled a chair up to the window. The rain had turned to a fine drizzle, but the sky, despite the dull overcast, had a curious luminosity that hurt his eyes. The hard light was just what he needed. The week of rain had given the brick walls of the houses across the street a sickly color, and the banality of the curtained windows was distressing.

Actually, he hardly saw the houses across the street. He was surprised to find, later, that he had not even been watching the little tailor who had become their good-luck symbol. He was very tired. He had thought of going to bed for a few hours, but instead remained sprawled in his chair, his collar open, his legs extended, smoking pipe after pipe and dropping the ashes on the floor.

Toward noon he got up suddenly, and went to the phone, called long-distance, and gave the operator a Hollywood number.

"Hello . . . That you, Ulstein?" Ulstein wasn't a friend. Combe had many friends in Hollywood, directors, French actors and actresses, but he was not calling them today. "This is Combe . . . Yes, François Combe . . . What? No, I'm calling from New York . . . Yes, I know that if you had something for me you would have written or wired me, but that's not why I'm calling . . . No, operator, I'm not through talking. . . ."

Ulstein was an awful jerk he had known in Paris, not at Fouquet's, because he was not a regular there. But he was always prowling the sidewalks in the immediate neighborhood so that people might think he had just come from Fouquet's.

"Remember our last conversation before I came East, Ulstein? You told me that if I was willing to play second or third leads . . . to speak frankly, minor parts . . . you'd have no trouble at all getting work for me . . . What's that?" Combe smiled bitterly. At any moment now Ulstein would begin boasting. "Figures, Ulstein, no generalities . . . I'm not talking about my career. How much a week? . . . Yes, to play any part . . . But damn it, that's my business, not yours! Just answer my question and leave the rest to me. . . ."

The unmade bed on one side, the gray rectangle of the window on the other. Harsh white and cold gray. His voice, too, was harsh.

"How much? . . . Six hundred dollars? . . . Only for good weeks? . . . Good, five hundred . . . Are you sure of what you're saying? . . . Are you prepared to sign a six-month contract, say, at that rate? . . . No, I can't give you an answer today. Tomorrow, probably . . . No, no. I'll call you."

Kay would know nothing of all this. She might expect to find the apartment filled with flowers. She would not know that he had thought of it but had shrugged it off scornfully. Wasn't he right in wondering, a little fearfully, whether they would still be on the same wave length?

Perhaps he had been moving too rapidly. He realized that he had covered quite a distance at a dizzy speed in a very short time, a distance that some men take years to cover, others a lifetime.

He heard bells when he left the house; it must have been noon. He started walking, his hands in the pockets of his beige raincoat. Kay could not know that, except for the fifteen minutes it took to eat a hot dog at a lunch counter, he had been walking for eight hours when he reached the air terminal to wait for her plane. He had crossed Green-

175

wich Village into the Lower East Side. He had found himself on the approach to the Brooklyn Bridge, and for the first time he walked across that historic iron span. He looked down.

It was cold. The drizzle had slacked off. The sky hung low over East River, dark and thick. The river was slashed with angry white wave crests. Tugs screamed angrily as they escorted ugly brown scows up and down the river.

Would she believe him if he told her the truth—that he had walked all the way from the Village to La Guardia, that he had stopped only three or four times in a neighborhood bar, and that he had not put even one nickel in a jukebox? That was something he no longer needed.

Everything he saw about him on his pilgrimage through a world that was monotonously gray—the little dark men swarming like ants under the lights, the stores, the movie houses with their garlands of light, the hot-dog stands, the bakeries with their displays of nauseating pastries; the coin machines that played music for you or allowed you to play at rolling balls into little holes that rang bells and lit lights; everything a great city could invent to deceive man's loneliness—he could now contemplate without a sinking feeling, and without panic.

She was coming home. She would soon be there.

He dragged his last anxious hours through the semi-urban desert of Queens, a desert of brick rectangles after brick rectangles with their iron zigzags of fire escapes. He wondered, not how people had the courage to live in such rectangular anthills, but where they found the courage to die there.

The busses passed him, loaded with faceless people, all with their own dark secrets. And the children, darkly silhouetted in the grayness, little people coming home from school, reaching desperately, they too, for some sort of gaiety.

The store fronts depressed him. The dummies in the show windows, holding out their too pink hands of wood or wax in unappealing gestures of appeal, revolted him.

Kay knew nothing of all this. How could she? How could she know that he had been pacing the terminal building at the airport for an hour and a half, eying the other pacers, some as tense and as anxious as he was, others gay or indifferent, all waiting. He wondered if he would be as calm as the calmest at the last minute.

That last minute was the moment of crisis. He wondered if, when he saw her again, she would be anything like herself, like the Kay that he loved. It was more subtle, deeper than that. He had promised himself that the moment he laid eyes on her he would say, "It's all over, Kay."

She wouldn't understand, of course; he knew that. It was a sort of a pun. She wouldn't know *what* was all over —that there would be no more pursuit, badgering, walking against infinity, chasing each other, taking or leaving—it was *that* which was over.

Yes, it was all over. It was his decision, and it was the reason why his day had been one of anxiety and soul-searching. Because it was still possible that she was not yet thinking and feeling on his plane, and that she might not want to go with him. And he had no more time to lose.

It was all over. That phrase summed it up. He had run the cycle. He had looped the loop to come back to the point where Destiny had been leading him, where Destiny, in fact, had first met him. In the all-night lunch counter, where they had been complete strangers to each other, their fate had already been decided over a plate of sausages and a plate of bacon and eggs. Instead of asking why, instead of groping blindly, resisting, rebelling, he now said with quiet humility and without shame: *I accept.*

He accepted everything. All their love and whatever its issue. Kay, just as she was, just as she had been, just as she might be. Would she really understand this when she saw him waiting in the anxious crowd behind the gray barriers of the airport?

She rushed toward him, trembling with excitement. She gave him her lips, unaware that at that moment he was not interested in her lips. She exclaimed:

"At last, François!" Then, because she was a woman: "You're all wet!"

She wondered why he was staring at her with such a peculiar expression, the expression of a sleepwalker, and why he was dragging her through the crowd, making way with savage elbows. She almost asked, *Aren't you glad to see me?* Then she thought of her suitcase. She said:

"We'll have to wait for my baggage, François."

"I'll have it delivered."

"But I might need some of my things. . . ."

"So what?" He took her baggage check, gave his address to a clerk, and hurried her toward the exits.

"It would have been so easy, with a taxi. I brought you something from Mexico, you know."

"Come on."

"Yes, François." Her eyes were frightened, submissive.

"Greenwich Village," he told the cabdriver. "Anywhere around Washington Square."

"But—"

He hadn't asked her if she was tired or if she had eaten. He had not noticed the new dress she was wearing under her coat. She entwined her fingers in his fingers. He did not react. He was stiff, indifferent. Her heart sank.

"François?"

"What?"

"You haven't really kissed me yet, you know."

It would have made no sense for him to kiss her here, not really kiss her, but he did it anyhow. He was condescending, and she felt it. She was really frightened.

"Listen, François."

"Yes?"

"Last night . . ."

He waited. He knew what she was going to say.

"I almost called you back last night. Forgive me if I'm wrong, but all the while I was talking to you, I had a feeling that there was someone else in the room."

He did not look at her. He did not want to be reminded of the other taxi, last night's taxi. . . .

"Answer me. I won't be angry. Although . . . in *our* bedroom . . ."

He said nonchalantly, almost acidly, "There was some one else there."

"I was sure of it. That's why I didn't dare call you back. François . . ."

He wanted no scenes. He had gone so far beyond that sort of thing that he shrank from the hand that gripped his so frantically, from her sniffling, from the tears she was fighting so hard to hold back. He was impatient to be home. It was a little like a bad dream—the long, long road that never seemed to end because there was always one more hill to climb. . . .

Would he have the courage to face it?

She should shut up. Someone should tell her to shut up, someone else. He could not do it himself. She had come back, and she thought that was enough. She had no idea what a long hurdle he had cleared while she was away.

She stammered, "Did . . . did you really do that, François?"

179

"Yes." He said it maliciously. He resented her impatience. Why couldn't she have waited for the marvelous moment that he had planned for her?

"I didn't think that I could ever be jealous again. I know very well that I have no right to be. . . ."

He was watching the neon signs. He saw the all-night café where they had first met. He ordered the driver:

"Stop at the corner."

It must be a disappointing homecoming for her. He knew that she was choking back the tears, but he couldn't help it. This was the way it had to be. He said:

"Come."

She followed meekly, uneasily, tortured by this new mystery he had become for her.

"We'll have a bite to eat," he said, "and then we'll go home."

As he stepped into the lighted doorway, he looked every inch the man of mystery, the international adventurer, with his damp trench coat, his rain-soaked hat, and his pipe, which, for the first time in her presence, he had lighted in the taxi.

It was he who ordered bacon and eggs for her without asking what she wanted. He also ordered her brand of cigarettes without waiting for her to dig into her handbag for her cigarette case. He opened the pack and offered her one.

Was she beginning to guess what it was that he had not yet been able to tell her?

"What I can't understand, François, is that it had to be just last night, the night when I was so happy because I could tell you I was coming home. . . ."

She might have found that he was looking at her coldly, that he had never looked at her so coldly, even on that first day, or first night, rather, when they had met on this very spot.

"Why did you do it?"

"I don't know. For your sake."

"What do you mean by that?"

"Nothing. It's too complicated." He was very solemn, almost distant. She had to talk, if only to move her lips.

"I must tell you right away," she said, "unless of course you don't want me to, what Larski did. Like I told you, I haven't accepted anything yet. I wanted to talk to you first."

He knew what she was going to say. Anyone observing them that night would have taken him for the most thick-skinned, inconsiderate man on earth. All this was so unimportant in relation to the decision he had made, in relation to the great human truth that had at last dawned upon him.

She was digging into her handbag. It was an error of taste and timing. She was so anxious in her quest that he forgave her.

"Look." She held up an impressive oblong of paper, a sight draft for five thousand dollars. "I want you to understand exactly . . ."

Yes, of course. He understood.

"He didn't do this in the spirit that you think, really. It was due me by the terms of our divorce, but I never wanted to bring up the question of money, any more than I wanted to bring up my right to have my daughter so many weeks a year."

"Your eggs are getting cold. Eat."

"Am I annoying you?"

"No." He said it sincerely.

Had he foreseen the routine? Almost. He was so far ahead that he had to wait for her to catch up, for he had reached the top of the hill long ago. He said, "Waiter. The salt."

This is where they had come in. The salt. The pepper.

181

Then the Worcestershire sauce. Then a light for her cigarette. Then . . . He was not impatient. He did not smile. He remained as solemn as he had been at the airport, and that was what baffled her.

"If only you knew him, and especially if you knew his family, you wouldn't be surprised."

Surprised? Why should he be surprised? By what?

"For centuries the Larskis have been landowners, with estates as big as the Alpes-Maritimes. At one time the land produced enormous revenues. I don't know if it still does, but the family is immensely wealthy. They had an eccentric old scholar, maybe he was crazy, maybe he was just smart, I wouldn't know, who lived in one of their castles, just cataloguing the library. He would read all day, make a few notes on bits of paper, and toss the paper into a box. After ten years, the box burned up. I'm sure he set fire to it himself.

"In that same castle there were three nurses, three old women. I don't know whom they were supposed to nurse, because Larski was an only child. They were housed in the outbuildings, did nothing all day, and lived off the fat of the land. I could go on like this for hours, but— What's the matter, darling?"

"Nothing."

He had just caught sight of her reflection in the mirror as he had on their first night, rather unflattering, a little distorted. This was the final test; he need hesitate no longer.

"Do you think I should keep the money?"

"We'll see about it."

"It's only for your sake that I'd accept it. I mean— now don't get angry—so I would not be just a dead weight around your neck. Do you understand?"

"Of course, *chérie*."

He almost wanted to laugh. It was so nearly grotesque.

Her poor little love was so far behind his own, which he was about to offer but about which she still knew nothing!

And she was so frightened! She was so bewildered! She resumed eating with deliberate slowness as though to put off the unknown that lay ahead. Then she lit the inevitable cigarette.

"My poor Kay!"

"What? Why do you say poor?"

"Because I have hurt you a little bit. I hasten to add that I did not do it deliberately, even though I think that it was necessary. It happened because I am a man, and therefore it may happen again."

"In our bedroom?"

"No."

She gave him a grateful look. She was still in the dark. She could not know yet that the bedroom in question was already becoming part of the past.

"Come."

She fell in step beside him. June too had adjusted her step so well to that of the man that their haunches had moved as one.

"You know, you've really hurt me deeply. I'm not angry with you, but—"

He stopped her under a street light and kissed her. It was the first time he had kissed her out of pity; the time had not yet come for the other kind.

"Would you like to go to our little bar for a drink?"

"No."

"What about Number One? It's not far."

"No."

"Very well."

She followed meekly, although perhaps not reassured, as they approached their house.

"I would never have thought that you would bring her here."

"I had to."

He wanted to get to the point quickly. He nudged her into the stairway, the way he had done with June the night before, but only he knew that no comparison was possible. Her fur trailed from her shoulders ahead of him. The pale legs came to a stop on the landing. He came abreast of her, opened the door, switched on the light.

There was no welcome for Kay. There was only the empty room, chilly and in a mess. He knew that she wanted to cry. Perhaps he even wanted to see her cry. He took off his trench coat, his hat, his gloves. He took off her hat and jacket. Just as her lower lip was beginning to form a pout, he said:

"You see, Kay, I have made an important decision."

She was still afraid. She looked at him with the wide, terrified eyes of a little girl, and he wanted to laugh. What a state to be in for making such a momentous declaration!

"I know now that I love you. Whatever the future may bring, whether it should be happiness or unhappiness, doesn't matter. I accept all of it in advance. That's what I wanted to tell you, Kay. That's what I wanted to shout into the phone, not only the first time you called, but again last night, in spite of everything. I love you. And I will love you whatever happens, whatever I may have to go through, whatever—"

It was his turn to be perplexed. Instead of falling into his arms, as he had expected, she remained frozen in the center of the room, pale, very cold. Hadn't he been right to worry about their being on the same wave length?

He called to her, as though she was a long way off.

"Kay!"

She did not look at him. She remained speechless.

184

"Kay!"

She did not come to him. On the contrary, she turned her back to him, ran into the bathroom, and closed the door.

"Kay!"

He stood dumfounded in the middle of the room he had deliberately left in disorder, his arms outstretched, his love at the tips of his empty fingers.

chapter 11

For a long time he sat deeply ensconced in his armchair, his eyes fixed on the bathroom door. No sound came from behind it. As the minutes dragged by, his calm returned. Impatience and perplexity slipped from him as confidence enveloped him gently with its insinuating warmth.

It seemed an eternity before the bathroom door opened without any preliminary sound. He saw the knob turning silently. Then the door swung out and Kay was there. They looked at each other without a word.

Something about her had changed, but he could not tell what. Her face, her hair were not the same. She wore no make-up. She had been traveling all day, yet her features were relaxed and her complexion blooming. She smiled timidly, a little awkwardly, and walked toward him. He had a strange, almost sacrilegious feeling that he was witnessing the birth of happiness.

She stopped in front of his chair and held out her hands for him to rise. At that solemn moment they must both be standing.

They stood very close together, cheek to cheek, but they did not embrace. The silence hung almost tangibly about them. It was she who dared break it at last. She breathed:

"You've come home."

He was ashamed, for he had a premonition of the truth.

"I didn't think you would come, François," she continued, "and I didn't even dare hope for it. Sometimes I hoped you wouldn't. Do you remember our taxi in the rain and the last words I said to you at the station, words I thought you would never understand? 'I don't feel any more as though I'm going away. . . . It's more like coming home.'

"I was speaking for myself.

"And now . . ."

He felt her go limp in his arms. He was just as weak and clumsy as she was as the result of this wonderful thing that had happened to them, but he tried to lead her to the bed before she collapsed. She protested feebly:

"No."

The bed was not their place that night. The two of them were wedged into the big, threadbare armchair, so close that their pulses pounded in unison and each could feel the other's breath upon his cheek.

"Don't say a word, François. Tomorrow . . ."

Tomorrow with the dawn they would enter into their new life forever. Tomorrow they would be lonely no longer, they would never be lonely again. He felt her shiver, and at the same moment he felt a tightening in his throat like some old, forgotten affliction. At the same instant they had both looked back for the last time at their past solitude. And both wondered how they had managed to live through it.

"Tomorrow," she repeated.

Tomorrow there would be no more beds, no more bedrooms in Manhattan. They would need them no longer. Nor would they need a jukebox in a little bar. Tomorrow and from tomorrow on they could go anywhere, be at home anywhere.

What was the meaning of that tenderly mocking smile that crossed her face the moment the little tailor across the way turned on the electric light that hung from a cord? He squeezed her hand to ask the question, for words were no longer needed.

She stroked his forehead as she said, "You thought that you had passed me, didn't you? You thought that you were far, far ahead of me, and all the while, poor darling, you were far, far behind."

Dawn of the new day was not far off. They could already hear the distant sounds of the city coming to life. Why should they hurry? This day would be theirs, as would all the others to follow, and the city—this one or another—could no longer frighten them. In a few hours this apartment, this bedroom, would exist no longer. There would be baggage on the floor and the armchair that now held them in its embrace would resume its shabby role as just furniture for a run-down Village apartment. They could look back without fear. Even the pillow with its mold of June's head had lost its dread. . . .

The future, said Combe, was up to Kay. Either they would return to France, if she wanted to, and with Kay by his side, he would quietly take his old place on the Paris stage. Or they would go to Hollywood and he would start over from scratch. It didn't matter to him. Weren't they starting from scratch anyway?

"I understand now," she said, "why it was you couldn't wait for me."

He opened his arms to embrace her, but she slipped from him, and, with a fluid movement, slid from the chair. In the half-light of dawn he saw her kneeling before him on the rug. She seized his hands and kissed them fervently. She whispered:

"Thank you."

They could draw back the curtains all the way now, to let the raw, sunless daylight outline the bare poverty of the room. As the new day began, they, calmly, fearlessly, and only a little awkwardly because it was so new, began the business of living.

They were smiling at each other across the room, and he could find no other phrase to express the happiness that welled up within him except: "Good morning, Kay."

Her lips trembled as she replied, "Good morning, François."

After a long silence, she turned from him to the window.

"Good-by, little tailor."

They locked the door as they left.

E₄